THE STARTUP SQUAD

Brian Weisfeld and Nicole C. Kear

[Imprint]
MAKE YOUR MARK

New York

[Imprint]
MAKE YOUR MARK

A part of Macmillan Publishing Group, LLC
175 Fifth Avenue, New York, NY 10010

THE STARTUP SQUAD. Copyright © 2019 by The Harold Martin Company, LLC. All rights reserved.
Printed in the United States of America by LSC Communications, Harrisonburg, Virginia.

Library of Congress Cataloging-in-Publication Data is available.

ISBN 978-1-250-18040-7 (hardcover) / ISBN 978-1-250-18041-4 (paperback) /
ISBN 978-1-250-18039-1 (ebook)

Our books may be purchased in bulk for promotional, educational, or business use.
Please contact your local bookseller or the Macmillan Corporate and
Premium Sales Department at (800) 221-7945 ext. 5442 or
by email at MacmillanSpecialMarkets@macmillan.com.

Book design by Elynn Cohen

Imprint logo designed by Amanda Spielman

First edition, 2019

1 3 5 7 9 10 8 6 4 2

mackids.com

Are you thinking about stealing this book? Seriously? Think again.
Don't mess with the Startup Squad. We mean business.

For help with the business tips starting on page 161, special thanks to EntreEd,
The Consortium for Entrepreneurship Education; Stewart Thornhill, Executive Director,
Samuel Zell & Robert H. Lurie Institute for Entrepreneurial Studies at University of Michigan's
Stephen M. Ross School of Business; Deborah Whitman, Director, Center for Entrepreneurial Studies
at Stanford Graduate School of Business; and the Young Entrepreneur Institute.

Also by Nicole C. Kear

~~~~~~~~

The Fix-It Friends series

Have No Fear!

Sticks and Stones

The Show Must Go On

Wish You Were Here

Eyes on the Prize

Three's a Crowd

Resa raced up the stairs to homeroom. She hated waiting almost as much as she hated losing. So she leaped up the steps two at a time, burst through the door, and crashed into the shoulder of someone who wasn't moving at warp speed.

Both of them tumbled to the floor amid a shower of sketchpad papers. An oversize pencil case landed with a thud at Resa's feet. Resa recognized that perfectly sorted case. She borrowed pencils from it pretty much every day.

Her best friend, Didi, was on her knees, picking up her tortoiseshell eyeglasses, which had been knocked off. She pushed her long, chestnut-colored hair behind her shoulders and shot her friend a "Really, Resa?" look. Over the years, Didi had had plenty of practice using that look.

"Sorry, Didi," Resa panted, collecting the papers.

"Teresa Marie Lopez," Didi said, pretending to scold her. "Where's the fire?"

"The fire," said Resa, getting to her feet, "is in my gut."

"Did you put expired milk in your cereal again?" Didi said, concerned. "You should always check the expiration dates."

Resa laughed and extended a hand to pull Didi up. "No, I'm just fired up! For the announcement!"

Didi looked at her blankly.

"Ms. Davis is announcing the sixth-grade trip today, remember?"

"Oh, yeeeeah," said Didi. "Right."

The girls walked the few remaining steps to their lockers. Resa's was on the top row in prime locker real estate, which she was grateful for, because who wanted to crouch down clumsily every time you had to grab a notebook? Of course, Didi, whose locker was on the bottom row a few doors over, didn't seem to mind. But then again, there was a whole world, a whole galaxy, of stuff that Didi didn't seem to mind but drove Resa crazy.

An elaborate collage covered the inside of Resa's

locker door. There were photos of Resa with Didi, plus photos with her mom, dad, and little brother, Ricky. At the center was a photo of Serena Williams hurtling herself toward a tennis ball, her racket frozen in the moment just before it hit. Looking at that photo always energized Resa for the day ahead. So did the postcard taped at the top of the door, which her mom had sent her at sleepaway camp last summer. It read: "A woman is like a tea bag. You can't tell how strong she is until you put her in hot water."

Resa tossed her jean jacket into the locker and grabbed her science, math, and social studies textbooks.

"Maybe the sixth-grade trip will be to the art museum in the city," Didi said hopefully. She hung her hand-knit sweater on the little locker hook. The inside of her locker door was bare, except for a small mirror. She inspected her reflection, fixing a wonky wave in her hair.

Resa groaned. "I hope not. The art museum's more boring than school. All those portraits of old guys? Ugh. You seen one, you seen 'em all." She slammed her locker closed. "Maybe it'll be to the science museum, the one with the bed of nails you can lie on. That would be amazing."

Didi shuddered. "I still have nightmares about that."

"It doesn't hurt," Resa exclaimed. "Because of physics, I think. I'm fuzzy on the details."

Resa, unable to wait a second longer for Didi to fix her already-fine hair, shut Didi's locker for her.

"Hey," objected Didi. "I wasn't done!"

"Yes, you were," said Resa, yanking on Didi's hand and pulling her down the hallway. "Your hair looks great."

Didi started to protest, but Resa had let go of her hand to run the last few steps to homeroom. She could tell from the din that the classroom was beginning to fill up. So much for getting to school early.

Every morning, she rushed to homeroom to beat Val there. Every morning, she failed. No matter how early she was, Val was always earlier. Sometimes Resa wondered if Val slept at school, just to come in first every time.

Sure enough, Val was next to Ms. Davis's desk, stapling packets like the helpful assistant she was.

From the outside, Val looked harmless. She was tiny, even shorter than Resa, who was one of the smallest kids in their homeroom. She had flaming-red hair, worn in a pixie cut so you could see every one of her freckles and her tiny, pointy fairy nose. In her T-shirt with a blue-sequined peace sign on the front, Val looked as sweet as cotton candy. But Resa knew better. She was as tough as that bed of nails Didi had nightmares about. Whatever the competition was, Val was in it to win it. And she almost always did.

Val looked up from her stapling as Resa ran in.

"Late again, huh?" she asked with a smirk.

"Homeroom hasn't even started yet," Resa shot back as she raced to the seat she'd been sitting in all year, next to Didi's.

"You know what Shakespeare said about punctuality?"

"No, but I'm sure you're gonna tell me."

" 'Better three hours too soon than a minute too late,' " Val said in her most patronizing tone. Then she hit the stapler especially hard, as if to emphasize her point.

Resa started to tell Val that she was a minute too late in shutting up. Thankfully, at that moment, Ms. Davis gestured for Val to take her seat in—where else?—the front row, and she called the class to order.

Ms. Davis wasn't the most popular teacher in the sixth grade. A lot of kids thought she was too strict, but Resa liked her no-nonsense attitude. She talked fast, got to the point, and expected kids to deliver. Some teachers, with enough tears and excuses, could be persuaded to let things slide. This was not Ms. Davis. You could cry her a river about how your guinea pig died and you were too devastated to take the math quiz, but Ms. Davis would just hand you a tissue and say, "I've heard geometry helps grief."

Resa didn't always see eye to eye with her, and they'd had plenty of clashes, but Resa still liked her. Today she stood in front of the class in her usual uniform—a pair of black pants, a crisp button-down shirt, and smudge-free, black eyeglasses.

"Good morning!" said Ms. Davis. "Let's settle down, please. I want to talk to you about the sixth-grade trip and fund-raising project."

Resa, bubbling over with anticipation, tapped her toes, clad in red Converse, on the floor.

Ms. Davis shot her a "cut it out" look. Her toes froze.

"I'm excited to tell you that for the sixth-grade trip, you'll be going to . . ." Ms. Davis paused, enjoying the rare moment of silence in the classroom. "Adventure Central!"

The class erupted into whoops, cheers, and laughter. Resa could hardly contain her excitement. Roller coasters were high on her list of favorite things, right below tennis and high-stakes gin rummy. She'd spent hours researching the world's best roller coasters, and it was her dream to ride every single one. Adventure Central didn't have any world-famous coasters, but it had some good ones nonetheless, and she never got to go as often as she wanted because her little brother, Ricky, was terrified of amusement parks.

"Listen up!" called Ms. Davis. "This is an expensive trip. You'll need to raise the money to pay for it. So the whole grade will be taking part in a fund-raising contest. You've been grouped into teams, and each team will run a lemonade stand. All the proceeds will go toward the trip. Now for the really fun part—"

She waited for the chattering to die down before she continued. "The team that earns the most money will win VIP tickets to Adventure Central."

"What's that mean, exactly?" Resa called out.

"As always," Ms. Davis said, "I'm happy to take questions if you raise your hand."

Resa raised her hand and repeated the question.

Ms. Davis consulted a piece of paper in front of her. "VIP tickets include free concessions, signature Adventure Central T-shirt and sun visor, and a pack of four QuickTix."

Even Ms. Davis couldn't stop a celebratory cheer from breaking out.

Resa swiveled to Didi and grabbed her arm. "Indira Singh," she said, looking her friend hard in the eyes, "I must win this contest."

Didi nodded. "Okay."

"You don't understand." Resa shook her head. "QuickTix allow you to completely skip the lines so you don't waste all day waiting."

Didi nodded. "Sounds cool." She liked the carousel at Adventure Central and, if she was feeling daring, the Ferris wheel, but the prospect of riding a bona fide roller coaster made her queasy. So QuickTix were pretty much useless to her, but she could see they were important to Resa. And when something was important to Resa, it was important to Didi. That's what it meant to be best friends.

Ms. Davis clapped to get everyone's attention. "The contest starts this weekend. I'm passing out packets with all the info you'll need, including team assignments." She handed a large stack of papers to Val to distribute. "Do not—I repeat, *do not*—ask me to change your team assignments. There will be no switching. There will be no trading. There will be no changes of any kind made. Are we clear?"

There were calls of "yeah," "okay," and, from Val, a chirpy "Crystal clear, Ms. Davis!"

"Good," Ms. Davis said. "One more thing: Be sure to plan your stand ahead of time. The more you plan this week, the less work you'll have this weekend. If you wait until the last minute to get organized, it may not go so smoothly. I know some of you tend to procrastinate." Ms. Davis raised her eyebrows and gave the students her "you know who you are" look before finishing: "Don't procrastinate with this one." She clapped her hands together. "Okay, that's it. Good luck!"

Didi turned to Resa. "I hope we're on the same team."

"Me too," Resa agreed. "And I hope I'm not with Harriet."

"What's wrong with Harriet?" Didi asked. "She's funny."

"Sure, she's funny," said Resa, "and also totally unreliable. I mean, she's not even here yet. She hasn't been on time for homeroom once this whole year." She gestured to Harriet's empty seat by the door.

Didi shrugged. "I like her."

"You like everyone."

"Not true!" Didi felt defensive, even though she wasn't sure what was wrong with liking everyone. "I don't like Clyde."

"Clyde is a nightmare of epic proportions," said Resa. "That doesn't count."

"And that new girl—Amelia. She weirds me out."

They both glanced at the back row, where Amelia sat in her seat, staring straight ahead. She looked like a marble statue, with her pale gray, totally unwrinkled shirt, her perfect posture, and her straight blond hair tucked neatly behind her ears.

"She's so . . . ," Didi said. "I don't know—"

"Snotty? Stuck-up? Totally antisocial?" Resa offered.

"I was going to say 'quiet.'"

Val finally arrived at Resa's desk. She flashed Resa a smile and said "good luck" as she handed over a packet. She didn't speak the words *you'll need it* out loud, but that's exactly what her smile said.

The top page of the packet listed the members of each team. Resa scanned the page for her name. There it was, at the bottom.

LEMONADE STAND

INFORMATION

Group 3

★ Indira Singh

★ Amelia Grant

★ Harriet Nguyen

★ Teresa Lopez

"You have got to be kidding me," Resa muttered to Didi, rereading the list of names in hopes that she'd made a mistake.

"We're in the same group!" said Didi, beaming.

"Uh, yeah," said Resa, and then, lowering her voice, "but we're also with Harriet. *And* the new girl."

"Still," said Didi, ever optimistic, "we're together. Which is the important part."

"Look at Group One," Resa grumbled. "Val, Clyde, Giovanni, *and* Grace? It's a dream team of overachievers."

"You're lucky you didn't end up with Clyde,"

said Didi. "Or Val. Remember the science fair last year? You and Val were on the same team and nearly killed each other."

An earsplitting shriek startled the two girls. Before they could identify its source, they were being pulled into a sudden, suffocating group hug.

"Hi, Harriet," said Didi. Or she tried to say that, at least. Her mouth was buried in Harriet's fake-fur sweater.

"Best! Team! *Ever!*" Harriet squealed, giving them one last squeeze before letting go. She jumped up to sit on Resa's desk, swinging her feet, which were clad in gold-sequined sneakers.

Harriet was a hurricane of color. She sported neon-yellow leggings topped with a pink fake-fur sweater and a denim miniskirt that she'd doodled on in permanent marker. She was easy to spot, all right.

"Guys, this is going to be *amazing*," Harriet said, clapping. "I have so many ideas! We need a sign, obviously! Something big! And colorful! And shiny! Something you can see from outer space!"

"So you're thinking subtle, then?" Resa said.

"No! The opposite of—" Harriet stopped herself and broke into a giggle. "Oh, you're being sarcastic. I love it! Classic! You're so funny, Resa!"

"The sign sounds like a good idea, Harriet," Didi chimed in.

"Yeah, sure," Resa said, "but we can't deal with signs yet. We need a product first."

"Yes! Totally!" Harriet agreed. "I was thinking . . . cupcakes. Everyone *loves* cupcakes!"

Resa worked hard to suppress a sigh. "I was thinking lemonade. Since, you know, it *has* to be a lemonade stand."

"Sure, totally!" Harriet nodded.

"We should probably get Amelia," Resa said. "Since she needs a formal invitation."

"Resa, she probably doesn't even know anyone's name yet," Didi pointed out. "She's only been here a week."

"I'll get her!" Harriet exclaimed, sliding off Resa's desk.

As soon as she was gone, Resa dropped her head into her hands. "Two weekends with her?" she moaned. "There's no way I can take it."

"At least she's excited," Didi said.

"Oh, I know she's excited." Resa picked her head up and opened her eyes super wide, as if she were getting an electric shock. "She is! So! Peppy! And she has no idea what's going on! She didn't even know it has to be a lemonade stand? How do you miss that?"

She pointed to the front of the packet, with its large, underlined, bolded, all-capitals heading:

LEMONADE STAND
INFORMATION

"True," said Didi. "But don't forget that she knows everybody in the neighborhood. She can totally rustle up customers for us. And customers are going to—"

"Got her!" announced Harriet, pulling over a very uncomfortable-looking Amelia by the hand.

"This is Resa," said Didi, smiling. "I'm Didi. And you already met Harriet, I guess."

"Yeah," said Amelia.

They waited for her to say something else, but she didn't.

"Oh-kay, then," said Resa. "So here's the deal: We have to win this thing. I'm obsessed with roller coasters, and Adventure Central has some amazing ones."

Harriet clapped in excitement. "Oh my gosh. Me too! The Parachute Plunge! The Whirling Dervish! The Turbo Torpedo! They're amazing!"

"Right," Resa agreed. "Except that usually when you go, you waste half your day waiting in lines and barely get to ride anything. So I don't just want that VIP ticket—I *need* it."

Didi nodded.

Amelia chimed in, "Will we also be getting VIP tickets, or just you?"

Didi saw a flicker of anger flash across Resa's face. She put out the fire by jumping in. "Great! So we should probably read the rules, first thing," she said. "They're on the second page."

Resa flipped open the packet.

RULES

 1. The lemonade stand can be operated only this Saturday and Sunday, as well as next Saturday and Sunday. Hours each day are nine to five.

 2. The lemonade stand must be operated within the limits of the school district.

 3. Your total budget should not exceed twenty dollars. Each family in the group has agreed to donate five dollars to the stand to fund the budget.

 4. Students must plan and operate the stand independently. Adult help is not permitted.

 5. All proceeds go to the school trip.

 6. Whichever team makes the most money wins the contest.

"Saturday's not that far away," Didi said. "We don't have a lot of time—"

As if on cue, the bell blared, signaling the end of homeroom. The daily stampede out the door was led by the kids, like Amelia and Harriet, who had Mrs. Ross for science first period. She made you recite the periodic table if you were late.

"Wanna meet up after school?" Resa called to Harriet and Amelia, who were both halfway to the door.

"Can't," said Harriet. "I'm helping my mom at the salon today."

"Violin," said Amelia.

"I guess we'll just talk in homeroom tomorrow," Resa said.

"Yes! I'm so excited!" Harriet yelled over her shoulder as she sailed out the door. Her two high pigtails shook like pom-poms.

"We should probably—" Amelia stopped herself midsentence. "Sure, whatever."

Resa watched her shuffle out the door.

"Perfect," Resa grumbled to Didi. "One of them is unbearably cheerful, and the other one's just plain unbearable."

"Well, you know what they say." Didi hooked her arm through Resa's. "When life gives you lemons, make lemonade."

When Resa's alarm went off the next morning, she was already sitting at her desk, scribbling in her Idea Book. Her trusty schnauzer, Stella, dozed at her feet.

Every year for her birthday, Resa's mom gave her a brand-new Idea Book. They were always the same size, small enough to fit in her pocket, but the cover changed every year. This year's cover was Resa's favorite. It had a holograph lightbulb, and when you tilted the book up or down, it looked as if the lightbulb were turning on and off.

Resa got her first Idea Book on her sixth birthday.

"You've got so many ideas flying around in that head of yours," her mom had said. "Now you can try to pin them down."

Ever since, Resa carried an Idea Book everywhere. You never knew when genius would strike. Of course, sometimes it was hard to tell, in the moment, which ideas were genius and which were, well . . . not. When she needed a laugh, Resa would read her very first book—or she'd try to read it, because it was nearly impossible to decipher her kindergarten scribblings. The stuff she could read, though, was hilarious. There was:

bcm a tiga (become a tiger)

rtooor rake in gt pone (return Ricky and get a pony)

masen dat tooorn spanc too socolat (machine that turns spinach into chocolate)

And this one, simple and mysterious:

frt powr (fart power)

Okay, the Idea Book wasn't foolproof. But as Resa's mom liked to say, you gotta crack a few eggs to make an omelet.

Resa finished jotting down her thoughts in her latest Idea Book, then slammed it shut so she could get dressed. The sound woke Stella, who followed Resa around as she pulled on her favorite soft-as-butter blue jeans and a plain white tank top. This was her base outfit, what she wore pretty much every day. The only decision she had to make was which color sweater to wear. She opened her closet and considered the eight cardigans hanging there, each in a different color but otherwise identical.

"Okay, Stella, how'm I feeling today?" She brushed her hand past each sweater. When she got to the purple one, Stella barked.

"Purple it is."

She pulled the sweater on, then slipped on a pair of periwinkle Converse and a lavender stretchy head-band to keep her thick, tight curls out of her eyes.

Didi, who thought Resa's outfits were too plain, was always trying to get her to add some variety to her wardrobe. Didi had a serious love affair with tiny floral patterns. If an item of clothing had a flower on it, Didi was powerless to resist it. Didi was also a fan of skirts and dresses—which was useful for Resa, because it gave her something to do with the clothing her *abuela* gave her every Christmas.

A quick look in the mirror and Resa was good to go. It never took Resa more than five minutes to get dressed, and that's the way she liked it. Especially today. She wanted to beat Val to homeroom for once.

She didn't beat Val, but at least they arrived at the same time.

"Got your trusty Idea Book, huh?" Val asked.

"Yep," said Resa. "I was up early, taking notes. We are going to have an unforgettable lemonade stand."

"So are we."

The girls bumped shoulders as they both tried to walk through the door of homeroom at the same time.

Ms. Davis laughed. "I know you love homeroom, ladies, but there's no need to break your necks getting in."

It seemed to take an eternity for Didi and Amelia to show up. There was no sign of Harriet anywhere.

Resa beckoned over the girls who were there, then held up her Idea Book. She tilted it so the lightbulb was illuminated. "I've been brainstorming! I figured everything out!"

"Great!" Didi chirped.

Amelia had opened her own notebook, where she'd taken notes, too. After Resa's proclamation, though, she shut it quietly. She pursed her lips and readied to hear Resa's big plan.

Resa flipped through the pages of her book until she found what she was looking for. Then she slammed the notebook, splayed open, onto the table. Didi leaned over to read the large letters scrawled there: *Think outside the lemon.*

"Think outside the lemon?" Amelia said. "What does that mean?"

"It means," Resa explained, "revolutionizing the

very idea of the lemonade stand! It means blowing minds by doing something unexpected, something never done before!"

Didi nodded, her big brown eyes on Resa.

"And what does *that* mean?" Amelia asked.

"It means signature lemonade flavors!" Resa declared.

Resa turned the page, and Amelia leaned over to read the words:

"Tomato basil lemonade?" She said it slowly, as if she could taste the words as she spoke them—and what she tasted disgusted her.

Resa nodded proudly. "And that's just the tip of the iceberg."

Amelia turned the pages of the notebook and read: "Watermelon poppy seed lemonade! Tangerine licorice lemonade! Blueberry balsamic vinegar!"

Resa beamed. Didi bit her fingernails.

"Are these recipes for lemonade or for science experiments?" Amelia asked.

Resa crossed her arms in front of her chest and fixed Amelia with her patented "say that again. Go ahead" look.

"It's really creative!" Didi piped up. "It's just . . . a little, um . . . fancy?"

"Well, yeah, that's the *point*," said Resa. She grabbed a pen from Didi's case and scribbled a word in her Idea Book for them: *gourmet!*

Amelia pulled out the pen tucked behind her ear and wrote something, too, in neat letters: *Gour-ross!*

Resa snapped her book closed and spun to face Amelia. "You got a better idea?"

"Hey, Amelia," Didi interjected. "Did you know that Resa's mom is the founder of Lo's Doughs?"

"The doughnut shops?" asked Amelia.

"The *gourmet* doughnut shops," corrected Resa.

"Yeah," Didi said, nodding a little too much. "You have to try the doughnut holes! They're seriously amazing!"

"Hell-*oooooo!*" Harriet's voice called out from the doorway as she ran over to the desk they were all crowded around. She was in overalls with a blue-and-red plaid shirt underneath and her black hair was in two braids, topped with a red bandanna. "What'd I miss?"

Just then, the bell rang, and the stampede began.

"Everything," said Resa to Harriet. "You missed everything."

"Oops, sorry," Harriet said with a giggle, already on her way to the door.

"Are we meeting after school?" asked Amelia.

"I have tennis," Resa replied.

"Tomorrow, then!" Harriet chirped.

Amelia sighed, pressed her notebook to her chest, and walked out the door.

"That wasn't so bad," Didi offered.

"You're joking, right?" Resa replied, slipping the Idea Book into the back pocket of her jeans. "How exactly could it have been worse?"

"Oh, Resa." Didi shook her head at her best friend. "Never ask that!"

The next two mornings at homeroom went like this:

1. Resa announced a Big Idea.
2. Amelia announced that the Big Idea would never work.
3. Arguing. Lots of arguing.
4. Didi jumped in with compliments and jokes to stop World War III.
5. Harriet walked in, ten minutes late, just before the bell rang.

At homeroom on Friday, Didi came prepared. She handed Resa and Amelia each a piece of paper titled "Supply List," detailing what each girl should bring from home for the stand the next day.

"Resa, I know your mom has a fruit squeezer and also that fold-up table from when she used to do catering," said Didi. "That would be perfect for the stand. The rest of the stuff is little things like pitchers and tablecloths and stuff."

"Looks good," said Amelia. "But it's missing something."

"What?" Didi asked.

Amelia grabbed the pen tucked behind her ear and wrote at the bottom of the page: *lemonade*.

"Yeah, I didn't include the ingredients because we haven't decided what we're going to make yet." Didi stuck her thumbnail in her mouth and started chewing. It was a bad habit, and she tried not to do it, but when she was really stressed, it was the only way she could calm down.

"Look," said Amelia. "Even if the gourmet flavors weren't gross, we can't afford to make them. The ingredients cost a fortune and we have only twenty dollars for everything—including cups and ice and stuff."

Amelia cracked open her composition notebook to a page she'd dog-eared and handed it to Resa. It was a list of prices in the neatest handwriting Resa had ever seen.

"I stopped by ShopMart yesterday and wrote down some prices," Amelia said. "We need two dozen lemons, sugar, a big bag of ice, and a pack of one hundred plastic cups." Amelia did some quick math, totaling the prices at the bottom of the page. "That's just over twenty dollars. We'll have to lose a few lemons. And we definitely have to lose the expensive gourmet stuff."

"Amelia, this is great!" Didi said. "You've covered everything!"

Amelia's lips parted in a small smile, and she shrugged a little. "Thanks."

Resa didn't say anything. She tapped the toes of her emerald-green Converse on the floor.

"So," said Didi, turning to Resa, "maybe we should keep it simple? Do old-school lemonade?"

Traitor, thought Resa. But what she said was "Sure."

"Perfect!" Didi exclaimed, relieved to have finally reached an agreement on something.

"Perfect?" asked Harriet. Her head popped up between Didi's and Amelia's shoulders, her hair pulled into a high, tight bun and earrings made of blue feathers dangling from her ears. "What's perfect?"

"Not your timing," Resa shot back. "The bell's about to ring, and you've missed another meeting."

Harriet's dark eyes widened. "Guys, I am so, so, *so* sorry. I couldn't find the hairbrush. You're not going to believe where it was. Guess. Just guess."

Resa sighed. "We don't really have time—"

"In the fridge!" Harriet exploded with laughter. "Isn't that nuts? Like, how does that even happen?"

"Harriet, tomorrow is go-time," Resa said. "We're all meeting at my house at nine."

"In the morning?" Harriet asked.

Resa blinked slowly and tried to compose herself. "Yes, nine in the morning. And you cannot be late. I *repeat*: You *cannot* be late."

Harriet gave Resa a little soldier salute. "Aye, aye, captain."

Didi handed Harriet a supply list.

"Can you bring this stuff?" she asked. "And don't forget to make the sign. Make sure we can see it from outer space."

"Roger that," Harriet replied with a smile.

Resa pulled out an envelope containing the cash they'd collected from their families: twenty dollars exactly. She handed it to Didi. "Don't forget to get the ingredients after school—"

"Actually, I can't. I've got yearbook." Didi handed the envelope back to Resa.

"Well, I can't do it," Resa said, annoyed. "I have tennis, and then I promised my mom I'd watch Ricky till she got home from work."

"I can do it," Amelia offered, plucking the envelope from Resa's hand. "The supermarket's on my way home."

If Amelia thought Resa was going to just hand over the cash to her after the way she'd been acting this week, she was totally off her rocker. Resa didn't like the new girl, and she didn't trust her, either. She'd rather give the job to Harriet—who would definitely lose the money before she even made it out of school.

"It's okay," Resa replied, snatching the envelope back. "I just realized—I can do it later tonight. No big deal."

"Are you sure?" Amelia asked, her lips pursing. "Because we *really* need that stuff. The lemons and all."

"Yeah, I sort of guessed we need lemons for lemonade," Resa shot back. "Don't worry—"

The bell blared, and the mad rush began.

"Make sure you're on time tomorrow!" Resa called, loud enough to be heard over the racket of footsteps.

Amelia didn't reply, and Resa wasn't sure, but she could have sworn she saw the new girl roll her eyes.

Harriet replied with gusto, just before she darted out the door, "Yep! Ten o'clock sharp!"

"What? No! Harriet—" But it was too late. Harriet and her feather earrings were long gone.

Resa turned to Didi, her jaw hanging open in disbelief.

"Oh, Resa, relax," said Didi. "It was a joke." She chewed on her thumbnail for a second, then added, "At least, I'm pretty sure it was."

Resa didn't make it to the supermarket later that night. Her *abuela* stopped by and there was a big dinner. After dinner, her *abuela* cornered her to ask why she kept her beautiful hair so short and why Resa never wore the dresses she gave her and why, for heaven's sake, she didn't know how to dance. Finally, Resa's mom noticed the "Help! Do something!" looks that Resa was shooting her, and her *abuela* headed home. But by that time, it was too late to run to the store. So Resa decided she'd get the stuff first thing in the morning.

Except that "first thing" ended up being a little

later than she expected. She woke to Stella licking her face and gasped when she saw the clock read 8:43 A.M.

"Mom!" she shouted, shoving her feet into her red Converse, not bothering to change out of her pj's. "Why didn't you wake me *uuuuupppp*?"

Stella barked, as if in agreement.

"Do I look like an alarm clock to you?" came her mom's voice from the kitchen.

Resa groaned as she grabbed her jacket and flew out the front door, yelling on her way out, "Going to the store!" She didn't remember that she'd left the envelope of money on her desk until she'd gathered all the ingredients and waited in line behind a woman with about four hundred groceries.

"Oh noooooo," Resa moaned as the cashier counted her lemons. "I gotta—I left my money. Be right back."

She sprinted the seven blocks back to her house. When she threw open the front door, panting, the first thing she heard was Amelia's voice coming from the kitchen.

". . . and it's a big promotion, I guess, because now my mom's an executive editor, but the paper said she needed to relocate. So we did."

So that's why she moved here, Resa thought.

"That must be hard, leaving your friends," Resa's mom was saying.

"Yeah," Amelia replied. It seemed as if she wanted to say more but didn't.

Resa stepped into the sun-drenched kitchen and found Amelia and Didi sitting at her kitchen table, across from her mom and Ricky. Ricky was wearing a black wizard cape with silver suns and moons sewed on. For months now, Ricky had been obsessed with all things wizard. She knew he was only seven and she should give him a break, but still, it was embarrassing when she had friends over.

Resa's dad was spooning scrambled eggs and sausage onto plates, while her mom filled their glasses with orange juice.

Hearing Resa's footsteps, her mom turned. "Hi, honey. Your friends are here."

"Except Harriet," observed Resa. "Big surprise."

"Well, actually—" Didi started, but before she could finish, Harriet burst through the door of the bathroom, dressed in banana-yellow sweatpants and a matching zip-up hoodie. Her hair had been twisted into two tight, high buns that looked a little like horns.

"Harriet!" said Resa, startled. "You're here. And you're so . . . bright."

Harriet spun in a circle, then made a *ta-da!* gesture. "It's eye-catching!" she said. "And it makes people think . . . *lemonade!*"

"Uh-huh," said Resa.

"Sit down and have some eggs," Resa's mom instructed. "Your dad made them scrambled with cheese, just how you like them."

"Can't," said Resa. "I have to go back to the supermarket. I forgot the money."

"Teresa Marie," her mom said sternly. "You're not about to run all around town without any breakfast."

"I made chorizo," said her dad, forking a bite and waving it in front of her as if he were performing hypnosis. As he waved, he sang, "Don't say no to chorizo."

"Dad, please don't start rhyming," Resa pleaded. The man knew a hundred ways to embarrass her.

"If you sit, I might see fit . . . to stop," her dad crooned.

So she sat. It was pointless to argue with parents about breakfast, Resa knew. She'd been down this road before. She let her dad load up her plate.

By the time they'd finished eating, it was past nine thirty. Then her mom insisted she change out of her pj's and fix her hair, which wasted more precious minutes. It was almost ten when the four girls walked out Resa's front door.

Resa rushed down her front steps, well ahead of the others. She was trying hard to ignore her thundering heart and queasy stomach. The vague feeling she'd had since waking up, that she didn't have any idea what she was doing, was getting stronger every minute. Ms. Davis had warned them to plan ahead, and she thought she had been doing exactly that—after all, she'd been brainstorming for days. All she'd forgotten was the boring, little detail of grocery shopping, but now it was an hour after selling was supposed to start, and they didn't even have their basic ingredients yet.

"The devil's in the details," her mom always said, and Resa guessed this is what she meant. She had plenty of Big Ideas, but what she didn't have were lemons.

"Come *on*," Resa called to the rest of the girls, who trailed behind her. "It's *late*."

"And whose fault is that?" Amelia muttered.

Didi ran to catch up with Resa, her long braid thumping against her back as she ran. She inhaled deeply. "It's sooooo nice out. A perfect day for lemonade!"

She was right, Resa knew. There wasn't a cloud in the sky. The gentle breeze carried the scent of freshly cut grass. Even the sparrows seemed to be tweeting especially sweetly. But it didn't brighten Resa's mood.

"Sure, it's a perfect day," said Resa, "but at this rate, it'll be midnight before we have our stand up and running."

Didi laughed and hip-checked her best friend, hoping it would make her smile. It didn't.

Usually, Resa enjoyed Didi's positivity, but when she was in an especially foul mood, she was allergic to optimism.

Resa reached the corner and spun around to wait for Harriet, who had come to a full stop halfway down the block. Harriet was crouching over a rock, her face inches from the stone.

"*Harriet! What are you doing?*" Resa bellowed.

"*I found a worm!*" Harriet shouted back. "*He's adorable!*"

"*Can we turn him into lemonade?*"

"*No!*" Harriet cried dramatically, clutching the wriggling worm to her chest.

"*Then drop him and get moving!*" barked Resa. She turned to Amelia, who was a few steps behind her. "Can you go get her?"

Amelia sighed, then turned in Harriet's direction. "Sure. Why not?" she muttered under her breath. "I live to serve."

She walked over to the rock, where Harriet was saying fond farewells to the worm.

"You better get a move on," Amelia said, "before Resa totally loses it."

Harriet placed the worm back on his rock, blew him a kiss, and started walking.

"Who made her team leader?" Amelia asked Harriet. "I mean, was there some kind of election I missed?"

Harriet shrugged. "Resa likes to call the shots. I don't really mind. It saves me from having to worry about it."

The girls crossed at the stop sign, then walked straight ahead to Market Street. They were about to turn right to head to ShopMart, but Resa noticed a crowd two blocks down to the left.

"What's with all the people?" asked Resa.

"Probably a soccer game," said Didi. "The park's there."

But Resa could hear, distantly, a voice shouting through what sounded like a megaphone. And the voice sounded familiar. She spun on her heel and headed toward the crowd.

"Resa!" called Didi. "I thought we were in a rush!"

As they approached the crowd, Resa could make out the words being shouted.

"Icy-cold lemonade! Get a cup for just two bucks!"

She followed the voice, fighting her way through the crowd, until she came face-to-face with Clyde McGovern, whose mouth was pressed against an orange megaphone. His dirty-blond hair, which usually flopped over his forehead and eyes, was hidden under a red baseball cap with a logo on it Resa didn't recognize. Probably a hockey team. Clyde lived for hockey. In fact, she was surprised he made time in his busy hockey schedule to run a lemonade stand. But if winning a hockey game was Clyde's all-time favorite thing, winning anything was his second favorite.

"*Be the first to quench your thirst!*" Clyde announced. "*Get your—oh, hey, Resa!*"

"Clyde, can you not, you know, with the mega—"

"*You mean, you don't want me to tell the world that Teresa Lopez, our main competition, is here instead of running her own lemonade stand? Buuuuuuusted!*"

"Thanks, Clyde," Resa said. "Thanks a lot."

"Resa!" Behind Clyde, Val was running over from the lemonade stand, where Giovanni poured lemonade as if his life depended on it and Grace collected money from a never-ending line of people.

Val's black shirt had a silver-sequined star emblazoned on the front, and when she ran, it twinkled like a disco ball. "Sizing up the competition?" she asked, flashing Resa a wide grin.

Resa bristled. "What? No. We were just—we were walking this way to—to get more lemons. Because we ran out. From selling so much."

"But the store's in the opposite direction," Val pointed out.

Resa laughed too loudly. "True. That is true."

Turning to Didi next to her, she asked, "What *are* we doing here?"

The look on Didi's face made a deer in the headlights look relaxed. Didi was an absolutely awful liar. She opened her mouth to reply, but no words came out.

"We wanted to wish you good luck," Amelia said smoothly. She'd walked up beside Resa and extended her hand to Val. "May the best team win."

Val grasped Amelia's hand and gave it a firm shake.

"Thanks," she said. "But you should probably keep the luck for yourselves." She gestured to the line behind her. "We're crushing it with the pregame sales. And it's not even that hot yet! Once the afternoon games start, we're going to be rolling in money."

Resa looked behind Val at the grassy field, where she could see groups of kids in jerseys gathering for soccer games. Val's team had picked a perfect spot. Without even trying, the stand would have a steady stream of customers walking right by all day.

"Val!" called Giovanni. "Can you scoop ice?"

"Coming!" Val shouted, then, turning to Resa: "Sorry. Break time's over."

As soon as she'd jogged away, Resa turned to Amelia and Didi. "Still think we have nothing to worry about?"

"It'll be fine—" Didi started to say.

Amelia shook her head, pursing her lips. "Resa was right. It's game on. Let's go."

"Wait," Didi broke in. "Where's Harriet?"

In her eye-catching yellow outfit, Harriet was hard to miss. There she was, at the front of the lemonade line, handing over two dollars to Val.

"What's she doing now?" moaned Resa.

"I can't be sure," said Amelia. "But it looks like she's buying lemonade."

By noon, Resa had decided their lemonade stand was cursed.

Nothing was going according to plan.

When they finally got to ShopMart to get the groceries, the checkout person said she'd held Resa's bags for a while but then figured she wasn't coming back and had someone put everything back. So they had to collect the ingredients all over again and then lug the eighteen lemons, sugar, and huge bag of ice back to Resa's house. Finally—finally—they were getting started, Resa thought. And that's when they made a discouraging discovery.

The fruit squeezer was broken. And not a-little-bit broken, not all-it-needs-is-some-duct-tape broken. It was missing the handle. Which did all the squeezing.

It was useless.

"I knew my mom hadn't used it in a while," Resa said. "But I didn't know it was this old."

"And you didn't check it last night?" Amelia's blue eyes flashed. "Did you somehow miss Ms. Davis's whole lecture on planning ahead?"

"I was under *abuela* attack!" protested Resa. "She made me try on dresses! With stockings!"

The girls sat at the kitchen table, staring glumly at the prehistoric squeezer—all except for Harriet, who was energetically squeezing a squeaky toy for Stella.

"It's no big deal," said Didi. "Let's just use powdered lemonade. It's way easier, anyway."

"We can't," said Amelia. "We used all our money on lemons we can't squeeze."

Harriet scooped Stella up onto her lap and scratched her vigorously under the chin. "So we'll just sell the lemons, then," said Harriet. "It'll be like DIY lemonade! Who *doesn't* like to suck on a lemon?"

"Uh-huh. Or," said Didi diplomatically, "we can squeeze them by hand."

So they started squeezing. They stabbed the lemon

halves with forks and yanked the forks back and forth, mashing up the pulp to get more juice out. On the upside, it was a great way to vent frustration. On the downside, it created only more frustration. And it took forever.

By noon, they had one cup of lemon juice.

"It doesn't look like enough," said Harriet skeptically.

"Yeah, but don't forget the ice," reminded Didi. "That takes up a lot of room."

"Still . . . ," said Amelia.

So they kept squeezing.

"You know," said Amelia when she was on what felt like her two hundredth lemon, "if we'd known about this last night, it would've taken us ten minutes to figure out how to get a new squeezer, instead of spending all day squeezing lemons by hand."

"Oh, have we been doing this for long?" Resa's voice was thick with sarcasm. "I hadn't noticed."

A little before one, Resa's mom walked by and, seeing the girls elbow-deep in lemon rinds, offered to help. Didi quickly declined the offer.

"No adult help!" she reminded Resa.

"Yeah, but—"

"No buts." Didi sliced a lemon in half, and Resa knew the knife wasn't as strong as Didi's will when she'd made up her mind. Didi had never broken a rule in her life. She'd never even bent one. So Resa's mom didn't help—but she did force them all to take a lunch break.

"Mommmmmmm," Resa complained. "All this eating is killing our productivity."

"Maybe. But not eating will kill you. Period," Resa's mom shot back as she flipped a grilled cheese. "So eat."

By two thirty, they had enough lemon juice to make a pitcher of lemonade. Of course, to fill the pitcher, they had to add a lot of water. More water, possibly, than they should have.

"This isn't lemonade," said Amelia, taking a taste. "It's water with a hint of lemon."

"It's *subtle*," Resa countered. "Subtle is good."

"Subtle is also all we've got right now," Didi reasoned.

"So we're good to go," Resa announced, screwing the top on the plastic pitcher. "Just grab your sign, Harriet, and we'll head out."

Harriet, washing her hands at the kitchen sink, said nothing. Which really wasn't like her.

"Harriet?" Resa asked, a nervous quaver in her voice. "Where'd you put the sign?"

Harriet shut off the water and turned slowly to Resa. She was wincing.

"What now?" Resa moaned.

"It was my dumb brother! He used all my poster supplies for his Battle of the Bands poster! I tried taping loose-leaf paper together, but it all kept falling apart! What could I do?"

"You could have said something!" Resa snapped. "In the past, you know, five hours that we've been sitting here squeezing lemons!"

"It's okay," Didi broke in. "It's almost three, anyway. By the time we set everything up in our spot, it'll be time to pack up again."

"Let's just start first thing tomorrow morning," said Amelia.

"Are you kidding?" Resa protested. "We're just going to waste the whole day?"

"It's not a waste," Didi assured her. "We got a lot done."

"And we can make the sign now!" Harriet chirped. "Okay, Resa, we need all your stick-on rhinestones. And sequins. And feathers would be good."

"Are you making a sign or a Disney princess?" asked Amelia.

"I have some cool metallic markers and stuff," said Didi, reaching into her backpack for yet another perfectly organized pencil case, this one full of art supplies.

Resa rolled her eyes but gave in. She retrieved the biggest piece of poster board she could find, and the girls spread out the supplies on the living room floor. Stella patrolled the area, sniffing each marker.

"So what should the sign say?" Harriet asked, uncapping a fat golden marker.

"Oh, I thought of a perfect name for our stand," said Resa, pulling her Idea Book out of her pocket and flipping through the pages. "Here it is: 'Lick-Your-Lips Lemonade! Where thirst goes to die!'"

Amelia raised her eyebrows. "Seriously?"

"You got a better idea?" Resa shot back.

"Uh, yeah. Pretty much anything that doesn't involve dying," said Amelia. "Death doesn't sell lemonade."

"How about . . . ," Resa turned the page. "'When life's sour, feel the power . . . of Lick-Your-Lips Lemonade!'"

"It's good!" said Didi, drawing a border of silver-colored stars on the poster board. "Just a little long."

Harriet cocked her head to the side. "How about just 'Make life sweet.'"

"Ooohhhhh," said Didi. "I like that."

"And we can shorten the name to "'Lickin' Lips Lemonade,'" Amelia added.

"Genius!" cried Harriet.

Resa nodded her head slowly, picturing the words on a sign.

"Lickin' Lips Lemonade," Resa repeated slowly. "Make life sweet."

Stella, at Harriet's side, barked once, then again.

"If a dog likes your slogan," said Harriet, "you know it's good."

"I'm sure that's how all major decisions are made in boardrooms across America," Resa said as Harriet laughed. Then, turning to the girls, she said. "I think we're back in the game."

The next morning at precisely nine o'clock, Didi rang Resa's doorbell. Before her finger had even let go of the bell, the door was flying open and there was Resa in a white tank top with a bright orange cardigan sweater and matching Converse.

"Right on time!" Resa grabbed Didi by the arm and pulled her into the living room. "Did you see Amelia and Harriet on your way? Where are they? It's almost 9:01."

"I didn't see them, but I'm sure they're coming." Didi hung her jacket on the coatrack, kicked off her boots by the door, then plopped onto Resa's large red couch. She'd stayed up too late the night before and wasn't feeling particularly perky.

"What are you doing?" Resa pulled her back up to her feet. "It's no time to relax! We've got lemonade to sell."

"Well, yeah," said Didi, letting herself flop back down. "But not right now, obviously."

"Why not?"

Didi arranged her face into her best "Really, Resa?" expression. "Do you not notice that I'm sopping wet?"

"You showered." Resa shrugged. "So what?"

"With my clothes on?" Didi laughed. Resa could make herself downright oblivious when she wanted to. "Take a look outside."

Resa pushed back the curtains on the living room's bay window.

The day before had been magnificent. Today was not. Today was wet. Today was gray. Today was a day that Didi was sure people wouldn't stop to accept a cup of lemonade if you paid them to. That is, if you could even find anybody walking the streets.

"A little water won't kill us," Resa said. "What am I, the Wicked Witch of the West?"

The doorbell rang and Resa raced over to let Amelia and Harriet in.

Gone was Harriet's eye-catching yellow sweat

suit. Instead, she wore a rainbow umbrella on her head and a green slicker.

"Is that," asked Resa, "an umbrella hat?"

"I'm siiiiinging in the rain!" Harriet crooned, stomping her rain boots in an imitation of tap dancing.

"I want an umbrella hat," said Amelia as she and Harriet walked in and dropped their wet rain things on the mat by the door. "Where'd you get it?"

"Cam-Thu," Harriet replied.

"Is that a store?" Amelia asked.

"It's a cousin." Harriet threw herself onto the couch next to Didi. "My eighth-grade cousin, to be exact. She's totally obsessed with clothes and accessories and stuff. And since she's an only child, I get all her amazing hand-me-downs."

"I want a Cam-Thu," pouted Didi.

"Guys!" Resa clapped to get their attention. "Enough with the fashion talk. We're way behind in the contest. We need to get moving."

"Sure," said Amelia, looking out the bay window. "We can take the ark. I'm sure Noah can spare it."

Resa glared at her. "It's not raining that much."

Didi sat up. "I checked the weather. It's supposed to clear up later this morning. So let's just do the rest of our prep work until then."

Harriet had hopped up and was walking into the kitchen.

"Harriet!" Resa called. "What are you—"

But it was too late. Harriet had entered the domain of Resa's mom, and Resa could hear her mom asking if Harriet wanted some buttermilk pancakes.

"Ooooooh, that sounds good," said Didi, getting to her feet.

"Guys, come on, we have to—" But Resa knew she was no match for her mother's flapjacks. So they'd have a quick bite while they waited for the weather to clear up, she reasoned as she followed the others into the kitchen.

Harriet sat next to Ricky and poured buckets of maple syrup onto her plate until her pancakes looked like islands in a lake of syrup.

"You really like syrup," Ricky observed.

"I *love* syrup," gushed Harriet. "And I never get to have any. I don't remember the last time my parents made pancakes . . . or any hot breakfast. They both hate to cook."

"Well, they have other talents," said Resa's mom. "I saw your dad's art exhibit at the library. His paintings are beautiful. And you know I won't let anyone but your mom touch my hair. She's a miracle worker."

Ricky perked up. "Is she a wizard?"

"In a manner of speaking," Resa's mom replied.

"I've got to meet this lady," Ricky said, biting into a rolled-up pancake.

"Does she do makeup, too?" asked Didi wistfully. Makeup was Didi's guilty pleasure. The only makeup she was allowed to wear outside the house was lip gloss, but she'd collected a sizable stash of beauty products to fool around with at home. Sometimes she would stay up late experimenting in the mirror. It helped her relax when she was stressed out. And last night, she'd been in serious need of de-stressing. She spent so long at her mirror with eye shadow that she'd nearly perfected a smoky eye.

"Of course!" said Harriet, forking up a huge bite of soggy pancake. "My mom's really good with contouring and—"

"As much as I like contouring," Amelia broke in, "we need to talk business."

"Yeah," Resa agreed. She plopped a pat of butter onto her steaming pancakes. "We forgot to talk prices yesterday. I think we should match Val's team's price. Two dollars."

"That's too high. We won't sell as many cups," said Amelia. "We should charge a dollar a cup."

"Why stop there?" said Resa. "Why not just give the lemonade away?"

"The lower our prices, the more cups we'll sell," said Amelia.

"The lower our prices, the less money we'll make," Resa replied.

"Why don't you—" Resa's mom started.

"Sorry, Mrs. Lopez," Didi interjected. "No adult help, remember?"

Resa's mom mimed zipping her lips and throwing away the key.

"Think about it. If we sell ten cups, we'll have twenty dollars—instead of a pathetic ten dollars," Resa pointed out, her mouth full of pancake. Her mom really did make the world's best pancakes.

"Yeah, but we won't sell ten cups at the lower price. We'll sell thirty," Amelia argued.

Resa shook her head. "No we won't."

Didi chewed her fingernails instead of her breakfast. "I just—I don't want people to think we're being jerks, you know, charging too much money."

"It's a business contest," said Resa, "not a popularity contest."

"Sure, but popularity helps in business, doesn't it?" asked Harriet, who was adding syrup to her shrinking pancake pile.

"I guess we could try two dollars a cup," said Didi. "But if it seems too high to customers, we should lower the price. Okay?"

She looked at Amelia with eyebrows raised in hopeful expectation.

"Okay," Amelia agreed. "We can try it."

"Great!" said Resa. "The price is two dollars. Didi,

you add the price to our sign. And while we wait for the rain to stop, the rest of us can squeeze some more lemons."

"Oh goody," grumbled Amelia.

"I know something else you can do while you wait," Resa's mom chimed in. "This big old pile of dirty dishes."

It was still pouring at ten.

It was still pouring at eleven . . . and at noon, too.

By 1:00 P.M., Resa was so restless, she was bouncing off the walls. Or, at least, her tennis ball was.

The girls had moved into Resa's garage, which was the only place in the house Resa could practice her backhand. Didi had sunk into a beanbag chair and was sketching Ricky's bicycle, while Amelia did Sudoku sitting on the steps that led to the house. Harriet sat on the floor teaching Stella tricks. Or trying to, at least.

"Paw," she commanded, her voice firm. "Paw. Paw. Don't you know what that means? *P-a-w*. Paw."

"I don't think spelling is going to help," said Resa as she hit a beat-up tennis ball against the wall of the garage. Every time it bounced off the wall—*Bam!*—back to her, she hit it head-on. "She doesn't do tricks. She's a—" *Bam!* "—free thinker."

Hitting the ball over and over and over again calmed Resa's nerves. Unfortunately, it rattled everyone else's—especially Didi, who liked things nice and quiet. Every time the ball hit the wall, Didi clenched her jaw.

"I just wish this rain—" *Bam!* "—would stop so we could—" *Bam!* "—get out there." *Bam!* Resa grunted and lunged for the ball. As she swung, her racket accidentally knocked Didi's hand, so her pencil swerved wildly across the page.

"Oops," said Resa. "Sorry, Di."

"Can you—" *Bam!* "—uh, I mean, maybe you should—" *Bam!* Didi took a breath and blurted, "Stop hitting that ball!"

Resa caught the tennis ball in her left palm. "You're right," said Resa.

"I am?"

"Enough hiding in the garage." Resa tossed the racket and ball into a blue bin stuffed full of sports equipment. "I'm going out there."

"What if it's still pouring?" asked Amelia.

"Then I won't bring water to add to the lemons," said Resa, striding past Amelia up the stairs to the house.

Luckily, the rain had slowed. Not stopped completely, but trickled down to a drizzle. It was still drippy and cold, but the girls put on their rain gear, loaded up Ricky's red wagon, and hit the road.

As soon as they were out the door, they started arguing over where they should set up the stand. Well, Resa, Didi, and Amelia did. Harriet was too busy feeding a squirrel to voice an opinion.

"Val picked the perfect location," Resa pointed out. "They stand there, and tons of people just walk by."

"I know," said Didi wistfully. "Too bad they've already claimed it."

"So let's just claim the corner across the street from them," Resa ventured.

"We can't do that," protested Didi. Even the thought of an argument with the other team made her heart race. "That'd be really mean."

Resa felt annoyed. Didi was always so worried about what people would think. She never wanted to rock the boat.

"It's a risky move," said Amelia. "We'd be giving ourselves a lot of competition—the customers will have a choice of who to go to. But if we choose somewhere else, we'll get all the customers—we won't have to share."

Resa sighed. "No other place is going to have so much foot traffic."

"What about Market and Monroe? Near Shop-Mart?" suggested Amelia.

"That's great!" agreed Didi. "Rain or shine, people need groceries."

"Let's try it, at least," said Amelia. "It's not a good day for the park, anyway. There aren't going to be any soccer games in this weather."

"I guess you're right," said Resa, relenting.

They set up across the street from ShopMart, on the opposite side of Monroe, in front of an elementary school. The school was closed for the weekend, but it had a bunch of benches for them to sit on if it ever stopped drizzling. There was also a bus stop in the middle of the block, and Resa thought they might catch customers getting off the bus.

The girls put their table under a tree to get a little shelter from the drizzle. They arranged the pitcher, ice, and cups on top and hung the sign off the front of the table. Then they huddled together, trying to use body warmth to keep from freezing.

Long, cold minutes passed. Not a single soul walked by. Cars constantly pulled into the supermarket parking lot across the street, but nobody was on foot today.

"How do you know you have frostbite?" asked Harriet, rubbing her hands together hard.

"It's not cold enough to get frostbite," Amelia replied. "But we could get pneumonia."

"No one's getting pneumonia!" snapped Resa. She stepped out from under the tree to face the group. "Guys! Look at us! It's no wonder we're not selling anything. You all look like you're at a funeral."

"Let's turn the glum into fun," said Harriet. "Let's get the sun to come out by cheering it on! Like at a football game."

With her umbrella hat secured on her head, Harriet darted out from under the tree and stood by the curb, chanting and jumping: "Gimme an *s*! Gimme a *u*! Gimme an *n*! What does it spell?" She climbed onto the bus stop bench and launched herself off it, shouting: "*Sun! Sun! Sun!*"

Harriet cajoled the others until Didi and Amelia joined in. Resa refused, instead watching with her arms crossed over her chest. The girls belted out "Here Comes the Sun" and "You Are My Sunshine" at top volume. They performed interpretive dances simulating the sun breaking through the clouds. It warmed them up and was way more fun than moping. And halfway through Harriet's performance of a modified Shakespearean monologue ("Sun, sun, wherefore art thou, sun?"), it actually started working.

The drizzle slowed to a drip. Small patches of sunlight broke through the clouds.

"Oh my gosh, it is *totally working!*" Harriet shrieked. "*We are magic!*"

"Come on, let's move the stand closer to the curb," said Resa. "It's showtime!"

Before you could say *meteorological miracle*, they had their first customer: Mr. Steuben, who owned the pet store farther down Market Street.

"Top of the morning to you, kind sir!" Harriet sang. "How are those baby Djungarian hamsters doing? I've been trying to talk my mom into letting me get one."

"With all your brothers' reptiles, it might not be the best idea," said Mr. Steuben.

"The injustice is too much to bear." Harriet sighed loudly. "So what can we get for you today?"

"How about a glass of your finest lemonade?" he asked.

"Coming right up!" Resa announced, reaching for the pitcher. Unfortunately, Didi had the same idea, and her arm knocked Resa's arm, which knocked over the pitcher, which drenched the table, the table-cloth, the sign—and Resa. Amelia lunged for the pitcher and righted it before it all spilled out. Still, more than half of their blood-sweat-and-tears lemonade lay in a puddle on the ground.

While Amelia poured some of the remains for their customer and collected his two dollars, Resa erupted at Didi. "What are you doing? I said I'd pour!"

"You never said that!" Didi pushed her glasses up the bridge of her nose.

"Now half of our lemonade's gone! And our sign's ruined! Not to mention my second-favorite pair of sneakers!" Resa lifted a soggy foot.

"It was an accident," Didi protested.

"Guys," Amelia said through the gritted teeth of a smile. "You're scaring away the customers."

Resa sighed. "I'll go home to change and make more lemonade. Amelia, come with me. Didi, you and Harriet hold down the fort here."

"Okay," said Didi, and then, under her breath, she added, "Since you asked so nicely."

As Didi watched Resa and Amelia walk away, she felt Harriet's arm around her shoulder.

"Don't sweat it, Didi," Harriet said. "You have no idea how many spills I've caused even just this week. I knocked over an entire batch of hair dye my mom was mixing yesterday—right onto Larry's blue-tongued skink."

"Is it okay?" Didi asked.

"Sure." Harriet smiled. "And now it's platinum blond!"

10

Didi and Harriet were a team supreme. Didi stood behind the stand, scooping ice, pouring lemonade, and collecting cash. Harriet stood in front of the stand, getting people to buy lemonade. There weren't a ton of customers, but the ones they had, they served well.

Then Harriet had to use the restroom in Shop-Mart, and Didi was left to man the stand herself. Didi wasn't a fan of this arrangement, but there wasn't much she could do, except hope and pray that no potential customers passed by. She had no idea what to say if they did. Asking people to give you money just seemed awkward and weird.

As luck would have it, as soon as Harriet left, a whole parade of people started walking by. At first, Didi froze. She pretended to have something urgent to take care of on her phone. But after she'd let half a dozen perfectly good customers pass by, her guilt grew strong enough that she forced herself to say something. She focused on an approaching mom, pushing a toddler in a stroller. She seemed nice enough.

"If you're thirsty, you might want to try some lemonade," Didi attempted feebly.

"What?" the mom said, wheeling the stroller up to the stand. "I didn't hear you, hon."

"Oh," said Didi, searing with embarrassment. "It was—I was only saying, if you're thirsty . . . We, umm, we're selling lemonade. But it's okay, you're busy, so don't worry about it."

The mom smiled. "Maybe another time."

Harriet popped up behind Didi, seemingly out of nowhere. "Maybe this cutie patootie would like to try a cup!" Harriet cooed, turning to the toddler. "Do you like lemonade? Icy-cold lemonade?"

The little girl's face lit up. "Yeah! Yeah! Mommy, I wan' some! Pleasepleasepleaseplease!"

The mom looked from her daughter to Harriet, a

wry smile on her face. "You know just who to ask, don't you?" she said. "All right, we'll take one cup."

When the mom had crossed the street, Harriet turned to Didi, eyebrows raised.

"I know, I know," Didi replied. "I'm the world's worst salesperson."

Harriet put both of her hands on Didi's shoulders. "Dear, sweet Didi," she said. "Anyone who talks trash about you is going to have to deal with *me*. So stop talking trash about yourself and listen up!"

"But it—"

"Nuh-uh-uh!" Harriet cut her off. "I am a master salesperson, yes or no?"

"You are," Didi agreed. "You're a natural. As opposed to me."

"Okay, so you're not a natural." Harriet shrugged. "But you can learn. It's not rocket science."

"Rocket science would probably be easier for me to learn," said Didi. "Can we do that instead?"

But Harriet had let go of Didi and was walking around to the other side of the stand. "Okay, so pretend I'm a customer." Harriet straightened her back and strode past the stand.

"Ummm, hi?" Didi attempted.

Harriet stopped in her tracks and walked over. "First problem!" Harriet announced. "You're too quiet. Try it again, louder this time. And start off with something peppier to get people's attention! And more fun! Like 'Hey! Love your shirt!' or 'What lousy weather, huh?'"

Harriet backtracked and strode by again.

Didi spoke a little louder this time. "Hey, I like your shirt."

Harriet stopped with exaggerated suddenness and walked over. "Oooooh, zank you, zank you. Iz from Par-ee! Zat's where I live, you know. Par-ee, Frrrrrrance!"

"That's, ummm, nice," Didi mumbled.

"No," said Harriet, folding her arms across her chest.

"No, Paris isn't nice?"

"Paris is amazing! I assume. I've never been," Harriet said. "I'm saying no to your sales style."

Didi didn't like this role-playing game. She just wanted to go back to scooping ice and making change. "Can we just—"

"Don't worry!" Harriet interrupted. "All you have to do is make eye contact! Seriously, it makes a big difference. And you should be even louder. When you feel like you're shouting, you're probably loud enough."

Harriet threw her shoulders back and spoke again. "*Oui, oui*, Par-ee iz ze most beautiful city in ze world!"

Didi forced herself to look up and meet Harriet's

glance. "Yes!" she said, loud enough that it made her wince a little. "That's what I hear!"

"So! Much! Better!" Harriet jumped up and down, clapping. "Okay, now tell me what you're selling."

"So we made this lemonade? And it's actually really good. It's, ummm, homemade, actually. So, if you want, well, the thing is, it's only two dollars, which is actually not that much. When you think about it."

Harriet said nothing. She was trying to figure out how to put it nicely. "Say less," said Harriet. "I mean, say more, but with less words. Like this!"

Harriet reached over the stand and picked up the pitcher of lemonade, then smiled brightly. "We're selling homemade lemonade today to raise money for our school!" She gave the pitcher a little shake. "It's icy cold and delicious, too! Can I get you a cup?"

Then Harriet placed the pitcher back in front of Didi. "You try."

Didi repeated what Harriet said, word for word. When she was done, she groaned. "It's still terrible!" she said. "I'm no good at this. Can we please stop now?"

"Indira Singh," said Harriet sternly. "Did you give up when you were learning to use pastels in art last year? No, you did not! And pastels are super hard. Every time I picked one up, I was on an express train to Smudge City! You practiced with those pastels, and you'll practice with this, too. C'mon, let's hear it again!"

Harriet would not relent, so Didi tried the pitch again, and again, and again. In the middle of what felt like the three hundredth time, Harriet spotted a young woman approaching.

"Ooooh, perfect!" she whispered. "Try it on her! Just like we practiced!"

"Harriet, no—"

But Harriet had suddenly vanished, leaving Didi alone.

She took a deep breath and blurted, "Hi! I like your shirt!"

The woman stopped, looked down at her plain white T-shirt, then looked up again. "Thanks?" she said.

Didi was horrified and wanted nothing more than to clamp her mouth shut and stop talking. That would have been even more awkward, though. There was no way but forward. She forced herself to say the words Harriet had made her memorize: "We're selling homemade lemonade today to raise money for our school! It's icy cold and delicious, too! Can I get you a cup?"

The woman seemed to soften, then smiled and read the sign. "Two dollars a cup? It better be icy cold," she teased.

"It is," said Didi. "And it's delicious."

"Sure, why not? I'll take a cup," the woman said, fishing in her purse.

Didi had to stifle a giggle as she scooped a cup full of extra ice. She'd made her first sale, and it felt fantastic. Harriet stayed gone until Didi had the chance to give her pitch a few more times and make another sale. Then she came back, flooded Didi with compliments, and, to Didi's relief, agreed to take over selling duties. It was Harriet's specialty. She stood on the street corner and announced a flash sale of the best lemonade in the state for only two dollars a pop.

"Get it while it's cold!" she bellowed. Harriet didn't even need a megaphone. She had a set of pipes that could be heard throughout the neighborhood.

Every time she talked to a customer, she refined her pitch, adding adjectives to her description of the lemonade. By the time they ran out of lemonade, she was advertising "icy-cold, fresh-squeezed, local, and organic lemonade." She wasn't exactly sure all those details were accurate, but Harriet, as a rule, didn't worry that much about the details.

When the pitcher was empty, Didi checked the clock on her phone. It was 4:13 P.M. They were running out of time and needed more lemonade. Where were Resa and Amelia, anyway? It seemed as if they'd been gone forever.

She texted Resa, but there was no answer. So she dialed her number, but no one picked up.

"I'm going to run over to Resa's house and see what's taking them so long," Didi shouted to Harriet, who was petting a Great Dane down the block. "Watch the stand!"

11

When Didi got to Resa's house, the door was ajar. She walked through, shutting it behind her. Stella bounded over and jumped up at her knees.

"Hey, Stellabella," said Didi, stroking her gray fur. "Where's Resa?"

A second later, her question was answered. Resa's voice boomed out of the kitchen: "How was I supposed to know you already put the sugar in?"

Amelia shouted right back: "I was about to *tell* you, but you didn't give me a chance!"

With Stella by her side, Didi walked quickly into the kitchen, where Amelia and Resa stood on opposite sides of the table, a large red mixing bowl between them.

"That's your problem," Amelia said. "You always just do whatever you want without checking with anyone else."

"Guys," Didi broke in. Neither of them turned in her direction.

"Oh, is that my problem? Really?" Resa said. "Want to know what *your* problem is?"

"I'd *love* to," snarled Amelia.

"It's okay," Didi said, stepping forward. "We'll just add water." But Amelia and Resa had locked eyes like the cowboys in the old Westerns her dad liked to watch. It was as if Didi weren't even there.

"Your problem is you think you're better than everyone else," said Resa, narrowing her eyes. "You lived in the city. Big deal. Get over yourself."

"What is that supposed to mean?"

"Nothing," said Didi. "She doesn't mean—"

"It means you're stuck-up!" Resa said, leaning over the table. "It means you're a know-it-all who doesn't actually know anything."

Amelia's pale face reddened, as if she'd been slapped. She took a step back from the kitchen table.

"Resa!" Didi exclaimed.

But Amelia tossed her wooden spoon into the mixing bowl and wiped her hands on her jeans.

"I'm out of here," she said, walking into the living room to grab her jacket.

Didi followed close behind her. "Wait, Amelia, don't—"

Amelia slipped her arms into the sleeves of her light blue raincoat.

"You're really nice, Didi," said Amelia, zipping it up. "But sometimes you're *too* nice."

Before Didi could say a word, Amelia was gone. Didi stood, staring at the door Amelia had slammed shut.

Now it was Didi's turn to feel as if she'd been slapped. Could a person be too nice? What did that even mean? She just wanted everyone to get along and stop fighting, which was pretty much impossible when Resa was involved.

Resa was so stubborn. Inflexible. It was always her way or the highway. To keep her happy, Didi had to be flexible enough for both of them. Which, honestly, wasn't always easy. Or fun. But she did it to keep the peace. And now she was being insulted for that?

Didi felt her heart start to race and her fingertips tingle. She stomped into the kitchen, where Resa was pouring water into the mixing bowl.

"Amelia left," she announced.

Resa shrugged. "I know."

"So you don't care?"

"We don't need her, anyway," Resa said, dipping a spoon in the mixture and sipping from it. She grimaced. "Ugh, it's still way too sweet. Thanks to Amelia, we put in double the sugar." She poured in more water from a measuring cup.

"Resa, this is serious. Our team is a disaster."

"How are the sales going? How much did we make— Oh no! Don't tell me you left Harriet *alone* with the stand? That's a terrible idea. You better get back there. Hurry, before she destroys the whole thing."

"No," said Didi. Her voice was so loud, it surprised her.

Resa looked up. "No? No to which part?"

"No to all of it," Didi said. "If you want to check on Harriet, you can do it yourself."

"Didi," said Resa, with a little scolding smile like a kindergarten teacher might use with a naughty kid. "I'm fixing this mess. Plus you're better with Harriet."

"I'm better with everyone," Didi snapped. "But that's not the point."

Resa dropped her spoon into the bowl and looked up at Didi. "Why are you in such a bad mood?"

"I'm not in a bad mood! The problem is you. You're on some kind of power trip," said Didi. "You're being rude. You're not listening to anyone. You're ordering us around like we're your servants!"

"Is this about Amelia? Don't worry; she'll come back."

"No," barked Didi. "It's not about her. I'm sick of just agreeing with you all the time. I have opinions, too, you know."

"Oh, Didi." Resa laughed. "I know you have opinions. You are totally overreacting."

That was the last straw. Didi unsnapped the fanny pack full of money and tossed it onto the kitchen table. Stella barked, getting excited.

"You want to see overreacting?" she spit out. "I'm leaving, too."

Resa didn't say a word. She didn't follow her best friend or try to stop her. She just stood there, staring at the mixing bowl.

Half of the team had quit. The lemonade was ruined. And they were out of money. She slumped into a kitchen chair.

Stella walked over and licked her hand. Resa lifted the dog onto her lap.

"Think you can squeeze a few lemons?" she asked, lifting up Stella's paw. "Probably need opposable thumbs for that, huh?"

She pulled Stella closer to her and gave her a squeeze. "Well, then, you can just offer moral support. I could use some of that."

12

Resa walked into school Monday ready to apologize to Didi as soon as she saw her. But when she got to homeroom, Didi wasn't in her usual chair next to Resa's seat. She was in the chair next to Amelia. As Resa watched, Didi unzipped her jumbo pencil case and handed Amelia a pen—the black flair pen that Resa thought of as rightfully hers.

It stung.

Just when Resa thought it couldn't get any worse, Val plopped down in the empty seat next to her.

"Hey, Resa." The wide smile on Val's face made her freckles stretch out. "Didn't see you yesterday. I passed your stand on my way to ShopMart to get more lemons, but you weren't there. It was just Harriet, playing fetch with a Great Dane. Your sign looked a little . . . soggy."

Resa could barely bring herself to respond. She felt heavy, as if she had cinder blocks tied to her arms and legs.

"I was taking a break," she managed.

"At first, I thought the day was going to be a total fail," said Val. "Because of the rain and everything. But we just spent the morning texting and calling absolutely everyone to let them know about the stand, and then they all came in the afternoon! So it was actually awesome!"

"Great," Resa muttered.

Resa had never been so relieved to hear the bell ring.

The rest of the week was not much better. Didi sat next to Amelia every day, and Val took Didi's newly vacant seat, talking Resa's ear off about all the rides she planned to go on at Adventure Central—with her QuickTix, of course.

At least Harriet wasn't mad at Resa. On Thursday morning she bounded over, wearing a cherry-red sweater with a black poodle on the front and a red-and-black plaid pleated skirt. Her hair was in a side ponytail with a red ribbon tied around it.

"Doesn't this guy look just like Stella?" Harriet asked, pointing to her sweater.

"Yeah," Resa replied. The dog didn't look anything like Stella, but she was just grateful that someone besides Val was talking to her.

"I wish I had a dog." Harriet sighed, leaning against Resa's desk. "You can't snuggle a skink. Trust me, I've tried."

"What's a skink?" asked Resa.

"It's a reptile. Like a lizard but, you know, with a cooler name," Harriet explained, retying the ribbon in her hair. "My brothers each have one, and I have to wait for all the skinks to die off before my mom will let me get a dog. I have considered foul play, believe me."

"How many brothers do you have?"

"Three," said Harriet. "Larry, Joe, and Sam."

"That's a lot of brothers."

"And a lot of skinks. Depressingly healthy skinks."

"Well, don't do anything desperate to the animals," said Resa, laughing. "You can always play with Stella till you get your own dog."

Harriet jumped up and clapped. "Yay! I'm so excited for this weekend! When are we going to meet up to plan, anyway?"

Resa shrugged. "I don't think anybody feels like a meeting."

Harriet followed Resa's gaze to the table where Amelia and Didi were bent over Didi's sketchpad.

"Ohhhhhhh." Harriet's brown eyes grew wide. "They're icing you out."

"They're not—"

"Don't worry!" Harriet exclaimed. "I'm on it!"

"Harriet, no, wa—"

But Harriet was on her way to Amelia and Didi. Leaning over to talk to them in confidence, she raised her eyebrows and shot Resa a pointed look. Then Didi and Amelia were looking at her, too, which was really awkward. Resa pulled out her Idea Book and doodled to make herself look busy.

Before she finished her first doodle, Harriet was at her side again. "Okay, so I got the scoop. They are super angry at you."

"Thanks, Harriet. I knew that already."

"But they are open to peace talks."

"What does that mean?"

Harriet took the pen from Resa's hands and scribbled something in the open page of her Idea Book. "Here's my address," said Harriet. "Report to my house tomorrow night, 6 o'clock. And bring doughnuts!"

Resa checked her Idea Book to make sure the address was right.

365 Walnut.

Yep, that was the number of the little blue house in front of her. But could this possibly be Harriet's house? The racket coming from the open windows did not seem like your typical Friday-night-with-the-family soundtrack. The noises sounded vaguely like musical instruments, but they weren't being played so much as destroyed.

Occasionally there was something that resembled the whine of an electric guitar, and every so often, the voice that was screaming seemed to be almost singing. But if this was music, Resa had never heard anything like it. And she didn't especially feel like hearing any more.

So she stood there, shifting from one hand to the other the Tupperware holding her mom's freshly baked doughnuts, wondering what to do, until she heard a truly cataclysmic explosion of crashes, which could have been drums but also could have been demolition. Then, total silence.

Resa seized the moment and darted up the three uneven front steps to ring the doorbell. Then she noticed a handwritten sign, which read, *Doorbell broken. Just knock!* So she did—three loud raps.

After what seemed like a long time, the door opened. A tall, skinny teenage boy stood there, a curtain of black hair covering one side of his face. He blinked the one eye Resa could see. "What's up?"

"Hi," said Resa. "I'm here, um, to see Harriet? Maybe I'm at the wrong—"

"*Harry!*" he bellowed so loudly and suddenly that Resa jumped. "*Harry Houdini, get your butt down here! You have a visitor!*"

"*Who is it?*" came a voice, which was not Harriet's, from up above somewhere. "*Is it Winnie?*"

"*It's not for you, Larry! It's for Harriet!*" The boy was so thin, it didn't look possible for him to produce so much sound, but there he was, shouting loud enough that Resa could feel the vibrations of his voice in her bones.

Resa heard footsteps on the sidewalk behind her. She turned to find Didi and Amelia at the base of the stairs.

"Is this Harriet's house?" asked Didi.

"Unclear," Resa replied.

"*Haaaaaarrrry!*" the boy shouted. "*There's more of them now!*"

There was a squeal from the top of the stairs, followed by a stampeding sound, and then Harriet was pulling the front door all the way open and pushing the boy out of the way.

"Joe!" she scolded him. "Why didn't you let them in?"

"They could be serial killers," Joe said, shrugging. He shuffled up the stairs while Harriet flung her arms around the three girls.

"I'm so, so, so glad you guys are here! Ooooooooh, doughnuts! Yum!"

Harriet kicked the front door closed and pulled the girls down a narrow hallway cluttered with countless pairs of men's sneakers.

"Sorry about the mess. My brothers' band is rehearsing tonight. The Rancid Skinks have the Battle of the Bands coming up, so they've been practicing constantly."

"That must have been the . . . um, music I heard," Resa said.

"That's a cool band name," said Amelia. "And it seems to fit their vibe."

"Oh, they have a few different bands, with different names. The Rancid Skinks play heavy metal, the Rambling Skinks play country, and then there's just the Skinks."

"What do they play?" asked Amelia.

"Kids' music!" Harriet chirped.

"Those guys play music for children?" muttered Amelia to Didi.

Resa followed Harriet down the hallway, stepping carefully over discarded shoes and socks and a mysterious green thing half-hidden under a backpack. Resa could swear the green thing moved.

"Oh, watch out for Zappa!" Harriet warned. She bent down, reached her hand around the mystery object, and lifted it into her arms. It looked sort of like a tiny, prehistoric dragon.

Didi jumped back. "What is that?"

Harriet placed the creature on her shoulder, and it froze there, its little claws clinging to the fabric of Harriet's green-and-blue Hawaiian shirt.

"She's a blue-tongued skink!" said Harriet. "She's the baby of her family, like me. I've tried to put a little pink bow on her head, but she always shakes it off."

Harriet turned to Zappa and spoke to her in cooing baby talk. "You do, don't you, you wittle wascal?"

"There are . . . more of them?" asked Didi, trying not to shudder as she scanned the room.

She was not a fan of animals in general. They were so unpredictable, and they had a tendency to lick you, which was just plain weird. Over the years, she'd learned to love the family dogs and cats that roamed the houses of her friends, like Stella, but she drew the line at anything with scales. Reptiles, she thought, belonged in a zoo, behind glass. Thick, shatterproof, fang-proof glass.

"Don't worry," said Harriet. "Zappa is super friendly! Unless you're a cricket. Then you're dead meat."

Didi trailed behind at a safe distance as Harriet led the girls into a small, bright kitchen. Squeezed into the corner was a rectangular table whose mismatched chairs were completely covered in stuff—clothing, towels, sheets of music, paintbrushes, and a surprisingly large number of maracas.

With Zappa clinging to her shoulder, Harriet walked over to a door in the kitchen's far corner, opened it, and yelled, "*Mommmm! They're heeeeeeere!*"

Then she skipped back to the table and started clearing off the chairs by pushing the piles of stuff onto the floor. "Sit! Sit! Sit!" she instructed.

There was the sound of heavy footsteps on the stairs and then a woman who looked like an older, rounder version of Harriet appeared. She wore a white apron with red streaks staining it. Red liquid covered her hands and dripped onto the linoleum floor.

"Do we need an escape plan?" Didi whispered to Resa.

"Unclear," Resa whispered back.

"Sweethearts!" shrieked Mrs. Nguyen as she rushed over to them, leaving a trail of red drops behind her. Halfway there, she seemed to remember her hands. "Ah! Sorry, sweeties!" she exclaimed. "I'm with a client in the middle of a single process downstairs."

She changed directions, heading to the sink, where she scrubbed her hands quickly. "I gotta get back down in a minute, but I had to come up and meet you girls! I've heard so much about you!"

She dried her hands on a dish towel and flung it over her shoulder. Then she hugged them one by one.

"Now *this* is what I call a healthy follicle," she pronounced to Amelia, pinching a golden lock between her fingers. "Let me ask you this: Have you ever considered bangs?"

When she got to Resa, she pushed the curls back from her eyes and said, "Oooh, you lucky girl, you. Look at these magnificent curls! Just like your mama." Then she wagged her finger in Resa's face. "But I can tell you're not conditioning!"

And when she got to Didi, she couldn't help but stroke her long, wavy hair and sigh. "Gorgeous. Just gorgeous. But let me put a few layers in here, sweetheart. You won't be disappointed."

Then she turned to Harriet and pulled her into a tight embrace.

"This is my baby here, my jewel. You girls like it? My signature double Dutch braid, with a fishtail twist!" She spun Harriet around to showcase the intricate braid hanging down her back. "It takes forever, but I think it's worth it."

Harriet wriggled away. "Mom, you're crushing Zappa."

"Okay, I gotta go back to Mrs. Zangoli. In two minutes, that dye can go from Blushing Rose to Gazpacho. And you do not want a Gazpacho head, trust me."

She excused herself and headed down the stairs.

"Your mom," said Amelia, "is totally awesome."

"She comes in handy." Harriet slid into a seat at the table. "Let's crack open these doughnuts. They look sensationally scrumptious. What kind are they?"

Harriet peeled off the Tupperware top, and a sweet, citrusy aroma wafted out.

"My mom's experimenting to find their next

flavor of the month," Resa said, sitting down. "So she wants your feedback. These are blood orange hibiscus."

Didi sunk her teeth into a pillowy doughnut, and the explosion of flavors made her close her eyes and hum.

"These are unreal," Amelia said between bites.

"Teresa Lopez," said Harriet with her mouth full, "your mother's a wizard."

"I'll tell Ricky," said Resa. "He'll be thrilled."

Resa was relieved by their reaction. She'd brought the special doughnuts as a peacemaking gesture. It was hard to stay angry with huge dollops of blood orange cream making you sigh in contentment. She decided to seize the moment. She cleared her throat.

"I just want to say that I'm sorry. I was a jerk."

Harriet gave Resa a little thumbs-up. Didi and Amelia exchanged glances.

"And . . . ?" said Amelia.

"And . . . ," continued Resa, "I won't be. A jerk, I mean. Anymore."

"You have to listen to the rest of us," said Didi. She was sitting at the far end of the table, as far from the skink as she could get. She twirled her hair into a twist, then threw it behind her shoulder. "You have to hear us out."

Resa nodded. "I know."

"We're not just here to bring your ideas to life,"

Amelia chimed in. "We have ideas of our own. It can't just be you calling all the shots."

Resa opened her mouth to defend herself but thought better of it. Instead, she said, "Okay. So . . . want to figure out the plan for this weekend?"

"You want the good news or the bad news?" asked Amelia, pulling a notebook out of her backpack.

"Good news," Resa said. Life was too short to get bad news first.

"After spilling a lot of our pitcher, we sold the rest. That's eight cups of lemonade, so we made sixteen dollars—"

"Nailed it!" interjected Harriet. She was on her third doughnut, and Zappa, still on her shoulder, was staring hard at the pastry, clearly waiting for her moment to snatch it.

"I wouldn't go that far," said Amelia. "I mean, we started with twenty dollars, did all that work, and now we have sixteen dollars. Really what happened is that we lost four dollars and two days of our lives."

"Is that the bad news?" asked Resa. She hoped it was.

"No, the bad news is that we're out of lemonade supplies," said Amelia. "And we already spent our whole twenty dollars."

"So, okay, yeah, that is bad news," Resa said. Her mind raced as she tapped her toes furiously. "Nobody panic! I'll figure something out."

"We already did," said Amelia. She grinned with obvious satisfaction, then took a big bite out of a doughnut.

"Amelia and I spoke to Ms. Davis," Didi explained, taking off her eyeglasses and wiping them clean on her shirt. "She said we can spend up to twenty dollars more for this weekend—it just has to come out of our sales from last week."

"Hallelujah!" exclaimed Harriet. "We're saved!"

"There goes our sixteen dollars," grumbled Resa before she could stop herself. Then, trying to sound less gloomy, she added, "It was a good idea to talk to Ms. Davis. How'd you convince her?"

"It was easy," said Didi. "It turns out a lot of kids ran into problems like us. So she decided to adjust the budget."

"You guys are *lifesavers*," Harriet gushed. Then, lowering her voice so she sounded somber, she said, "But the time has come for us to discuss something serious."

Perfect, Resa thought. *Just what we need. Harriet drama.*

"I've been thinking . . ." Harriet lingered a moment, enjoying having everyone's attention. She let Zappa lick the sugar off her finger. Didi, terrified, could not rip her eyes away from her long, darting tongue. It was, as the name promised, blue.

"We need to lower our prices!" Harriet announced.

"Oh, come on," Resa protested. "We already decided on two dollars."

"We decided to *try* two dollars," said Amelia, "and lower it later if we had to."

"Last weekend, lots of people were going to buy a cup," Harriet went on, "until I told them the price."

"Val's team doesn't have a problem selling cups for two dollars," Resa pointed out.

"Yeah, well, Val's team has a lot of stuff going for it that we don't," said Amelia.

Resa's heart pounded in her chest. She wanted to yell, "Nobody asked you!" and shut Amelia up once and for all. But just a minute ago, she'd promised to listen to everyone's input. *No matter how dumb*, she thought.

"We can just lower the price a little," suggested Amelia. "To one dollar fifty."

Resa bit her lip as she considered this. "That could be good. I bet some adults will give us two dollars and tell us just to keep the change."

"Exactly," said Amelia.

"Okay, fine," Resa agreed. "But listen, guys, it doesn't matter how low our prices are if there are no customers around. Our location is no good. We need to move."

"Maybe we're too far from ShopMart," said Amelia. "We could set up right out front."

"I'll grab people as they're walking in and out!" Harriet promised.

Resa had been thinking they could move over to the park, where there was a never-ending line of thirsty soccer players and their families. But she had just promised to listen to the others, and maybe it would work to be right in front of ShopMart. There were always people there.

"I guess we can try it," said Resa begrudgingly.

"This time," Didi said, "we'll have to use powdered lemonade. It's way cheaper than fresh lemons, and it makes a lot more lemonade, too."

"Definitely!" said Harriet. She held up the index finger on her left hand. "I got a paper cut yesterday. There's no way I'm putting lemons anywhere near this baby. No way!"

Resa sighed. "I wanted to make homemade lemonade, not that instant stuff."

"This isn't a lemonade-recipe contest," said Amelia. "It's a lemonade-selling contest. We're trying to sell the most lemonade, not create the best recipe."

"Plus," added Didi, "we don't have any other choice. So . . . is it a plan?"

Resa looked at her best friend's hopeful face and realized how much she'd missed her this past week. She knew she wasn't always the easiest person to get along with, and she really did want to be a little easier. She figured she could start with powdered lemonade.

"Okay," said Resa. "I think all we need now is a new sign. The last one didn't survive the spill."

"I'll do it!" said Harriet.

Resa tried not to let the doubt she was feeling show on her face. It wasn't easy.

"Do you . . . want any help?" she asked.

"Nope!" chirped Harriet. "I've got it all under control."

Resa clamped her lips shut. As hard as it was, she'd just have to trust Harriet. Flighty, unreliable Harriet.

"Okay, then!" said Resa with forced cheer. "I guess we're all set!"

The cheerfulness was contagious—dangerously so. It triggered a squeal from Harriet, followed by: "*We're gonna wiiiiiiin!*" This startled Zappa, who leaped from Harriet's shoulder onto the kitchen table, which she crossed in under two seconds. Before Didi could get to her feet, the skink had run up her arm and scrambled onto her head.

"*Get it off of me!*" shrieked Didi, flailing her limbs wildly. The more she flailed, the harder Zappa hung on. By the time Harriet reached her, Didi's long hair had gotten completely tangled around Zappa's claws. No one could get her loose until Harriet called her oldest brother, Sam, who lured Zappa off Didi's head with an especially juicy cricket.

"I'm really sorry about the Zappa attack-a," said Harriet, placing her arm around Didi's shoulder.

"Uh-huh," sniffed Didi, still shaking.

Later, as the girls walked down Walnut Street toward their homes, Resa asked Didi and Amelia, "Are we all good?"

"Sure," Amelia replied.

"Under one condition," Didi said, smoothing down her tangled hair. "Promise me we will never, ever have another meeting at Harriet's house."

14

The next morning, Resa stood in front of Shop-Mart's automatic sliding doors five full minutes before the store opened. She leaned against the store window and tapped the toes of her electric-blue Converse until, finally, a woman wearing a Shop-Mart vest unlocked the doors. As soon as they glided open, Resa was through the doorway. She ran down the fruit aisle, through the frozen-food section, and up the aisle that housed assorted juices and drinks. There, just above her head, she found the shelf for instant lemonade.

It was empty.

Resa stood on tiptoes and reached way back on the shelf until her fingers hit the wall.

Nothing.

"Excuse me!" she called up the aisle to the saleswoman who'd opened the doors for her. "Where's your powdered lemonade?"

The woman frowned. "You too?"

"Huh?" asked Resa.

"What's with the lemonade craze? All week, we've been overrun by kids desperate for something, anything, to make lemonade out of." She smirked. "Is there some kind of lemonade festival going on?"

"So you're all out?" Resa asked.

The saleswoman nodded. "Out of lemons, too. But we'll get more of both—maybe tomorrow."

Resa slumped her shoulders and groaned loudly.

"Me, personally, I prefer apple juice," said the saleswoman. "And it's on sale this week."

Resa shook her head. "It's got to be lemonade."

The saleswoman shrugged. "Check Harris Fullers. It won't be cheap, but they might have some."

"Thanks!" Resa yelled over her shoulder as she sprinted out of the store. She pounded the pavement, pumping her arms, and made it home in five minutes. She hated doing conditioning in tennis, but she had to admit, it paid off sometimes.

Resa raced up the stairs and into her parents' bedroom, where she found Ricky and her mom, still in their pj's, snuggled up in bed, reading—what else?—Ricky's massive book of wizard spells.

Resa ran over to the bed, shut the book, and hefted it out of their hands. It took both hands. The thing was enormous.

"Lemonade emergency!" Resa pronounced. "C'mon, c'mon, c'mon."

"Am I hallucinating, or did she just snatch that right out of my hand?" Resa's mom asked Ricky.

"*Taceo! Nova figura!*" Ricky shouted, pointing his finger at her. "*Et e eruca figura!*"

"Cut it out, Ricky!" Resa snapped. And then, after considering for a second, she asked, "What does that mean?"

"I turned you into a caterpillar."

"Can you turn me into a cheetah instead?" Resa replied. "I need to move fast."

~~~~~

It took Resa what felt like an eternity to explain to her mom what was going on, but finally, *finally*, her mom agreed to drive her to Harris Fullers. At first, Resa's mom wanted to get dressed and have some coffee. Resa nearly burst into tears at the prospect of getting another late start, so her mom took pity on her and got into the car wearing her pj's.

~~~~~

The good news was that Harris Fullers had powdered lemonade. The bad news was that it cost double what Resa would have paid at ShopMart. With sixteen dollars, after buying the ice they needed, all she could afford was a small container. Still, it was way better than nothing. Plus, back at home, Resa discovered the other girls were right—the powdered lemonade was so easy to make, it felt like magic. Gone were the hours of finger-aching lemon-wringing, which produced a few measly drops of juice. Gone was the mess and stress of adding sugar. With the instant stuff, Resa just added water and *presto chango!* she had a full pitcher of lemonade.

When Didi rang her doorbell at 9:00 A.M., Resa threw her arms around her best friend.

"Somebody's cheerful," Didi teased, but really, she was relieved. Resa's glum moods were zero fun, but when she was in high spirits, there was no one better to spend time with.

"I have a good feeling about today," Resa said. "I think our luck is gonna change."

By nine thirty, Lickin' Lips Lemonade was up and running on the corner of Market and Monroe. This time, they'd positioned themselves right next to the ShopMart entrance.

They'd finished setting up the stand—tablecloth, ice bucket, and all—when Harriet finally showed up in green biker shorts and a tiger-print tank top. Resa had to squeeze her fists into balls to resist the urge to holler at her for being late, but she knew she shouldn't start the day off like that, not after last week's blowout. Plus, Harriet wasn't empty-handed. She was holding the biggest piece of rolled-up poster board Resa had ever seen. Didi, Amelia, and Resa had watched her walk up Market Street holding it. She'd accidentally whacked two dogs and three toddlers with it.

"Is that our new sign?" asked Amelia. "Or a weapon of mass destruction?"

Harriet beamed. "You guys are going to freak out. Are you ready?"

"Uh-huh," said Resa, although the truth was, when it came to Harriet's surprises, no one was ever ready. The best you could do was expect the unexpected.

It took three of them to unroll the sign. When it stood upright, it reached Resa's shoulders. The uneven letters were written in silver spray paint, and it was bordered with stars cut out of aluminum foil. From the looks of it, half of them had fallen off or been torn.

"It's . . ." Resa took a deep breath and tried to choose her words carefully. "It's great, Harriet. I'm 99 percent sure you can see this one from space."

"Or at least from very high altitudes," added Amelia.

With plenty of tape, they managed to hang the sign on the brick wall next to the ShopMart entrance. Then they waited.

Amelia had been right. ShopMart was packed with people, and the parking lot was mostly full all morning. ShopMart had a steady stream of customers that never seemed to slow. But hardly any of them stopped at Lickin' Lips Lemonade. Plenty noticed the sign, wished them luck, and even complimented their business name and slogan. Which was all well and good, but compliments don't win QuickTix.

The stand got a few customers—mostly kids who were shopping with their parents and wouldn't stop pestering them until Mom or Dad said, "Fine, all right," and coughed up $1.50. But that was only every so often. After three hours, they'd sold only thirteen cups.

Slowly but surely, Resa had gone from cheerful to concerned to crabby. She was about to jump out of her skin with frustration. To keep from exploding, she did jumping jacks.

Didi sat cross-legged on the ground, while Harriet French-braided her long hair. Amelia leaned against the brick wall, her arms crossed over her chest.

"I don't get it," Amelia said. "The store is packed with people. Why aren't we selling more lemonade?"

"Maybe we smell," said Harriet. "Sniff your armpits, everyone!"

"We don't smell," said Resa as she jumped. "The problem is, everyone here is shopping. So they don't want to buy a cup on their way in, because they can't take it into the store, and when they come out, their hands are full of bags."

"Look on the bright side!" said Didi as Harriet

tugged at her hair. "We sold more cups than last weekend! Almost double!"

"Yeah, but double terrible is not great," said Resa as she did some leg lunges. "Double terrible is just less terrible."

"I'm just trying to make the best out of it," said Didi.

Resa stopped lunging and faced the girls. "We're in the wrong location. We should move."

Didi looked worried. Harriet moaned.

"That'll take soooooo much work. And time, too," Harriet protested. "We don't want to waste precious minutes relocating when we could be selling!"

Resa knew Harriet didn't really care about wasting time. She just didn't want the hassle of packing and unpacking.

"Anyway, it's my fault we haven't sold more," said Harriet, tying off the braid with a rubber band. "I should be getting more customers. Fear not! I will try harder!"

And she did. Harriet created and performed a jingle for the stand, sang to the tune of "Tomorrow" from *Annie*.

"Lemonade! Lemonade!
"I love ya, lemonade!
"There's some for you riiiight here!"

A few adults, especially the grandparent types,

seemed to like this, and Harriet, encouraged, made up a tap dance to go with it. She didn't appear to have lots of experience in tap, but it was upbeat and funny, and they sold a few more cups of lemonade.

Tired from the singing and dancing, Harriet resorted to leaning against the wall next to Amelia, making announcements. At first, these were unobjectionable.

"Thirsty? Treat yourself to a *refreshing* cup of *icy-cold* lemonaaaaaaade!"

But when her sales pitch didn't have the result she wanted, Harriet started to get frustrated.

"What's wrong with these people?" she grumbled to no one in particular. Then, cupping her hands around her mouth, she yelled: "Folks! The lemonade is *delicious*! And it's *only* one dollar!"

"One dollar fifty," Didi corrected.

"It doesn't matter anyway, because *no one will even bother to stop!*" Harriet shouted directly at a family walking past them to the parking lot.

Resa rose to her feet, ready to tell Harriet to back off. Harriet needed a break or she'd totally short-circuit. But as Resa opened her mouth to cut Harriet off, she remembered her promise to listen more and order people around less. Maybe she shouldn't be the one always jumping in first. She closed her mouth and hoped Harriet would just cool down on her own.

Instead, Harriet heated up even more.

"Seriously?" she shouted. "No one wants to help kids in *need*?"

Didi interjected: "I mean, we're not really in—"

"*People!* We're just trying to make a living here!" Harriet was gesticulating wildly now, lost in the moment. "*It's just one measly buck! How hard-hearted can you be?*"

Didi shot Resa a pleading look that said, "Hey, leader! Do some leading!" It was all Resa needed to jump into action.

"Okay, that's it," said Resa, putting an arm around Harriet's shoulders. Harriet stomped loudly as Resa led her around the corner to a quiet side street.

"You need a break," Resa said.

"Why?" Harriet snarled. "You think I'm doing a bad job?"

Resa said nothing.

"I've sold a ton of lemonade for this stand!" Harriet huffed. "And this is the thanks I get!"

"I think you're just tired," said Resa. "You've been working all morning. Take a break."

Harriet shrugged. "I *am* hungry."

"Exactly."

Resa was relieved when Harriet skipped off to take a break, promising to be back in ten minutes. Fifteen, at most.

"Where is she?" asked Resa. She paced in front of the stand, walking nonstop and getting nowhere. Harriet had been gone an hour and a half, and there was no sign of her anywhere.

"Should we call her?" asked Didi. She was sitting next to Amelia, their backs against the wall of ShopMart, Didi's collection of lip gloss lined up in front of them. Out of sheer boredom, Didi had given Amelia the full, unabridged lip-gloss tour, letting her try each one.

"We can't call her," said Resa in exasperation. "She doesn't have a phone."

Resa had a terrible feeling that she'd made a mistake by sending Harriet off to take a break. Who knew where she went or when she'd be back? On the other hand, what else could Resa have done? Let Harriet berate the customers?

"I'm sure she's just lost track of time," said Amelia, spreading a coral gloss over her lips. "Has she ever been on time for anything?"

Didi tossed the glosses into her backpack and got to her feet. "I'm going to ask if I can use the bathroom inside ShopMart. Anyone want anything?"

"Yeah," said Resa. "Check the drinks aisle to see if they have any powdered lemonade. We're down to our last cup."

"Sure," said Didi as she disappeared through the automatic doors.

"How can we be out of lemonade?" Amelia asked. "We made only three pitchers. A container makes way more than that."

"Not this container," said Resa, fishing around in the red wagon to find the empty lemonade tub.

"*That's* what you bought this morning?" asked Amelia. "It's tiny! It belongs in a dollhouse!"

Resa rolled her eyes. "Harris Fullers is expensive, Amelia. This cost ten seventy-five. Then I had to buy the ice. It was all we could afford."

"Why'd you go to *Harris Fullers*?" Amelia asked.

She didn't say, *Are you stupid?* but Resa heard that message come through loud and clear

Resa felt her face start to flush with anger. *Typical Amelia, jumping to conclusions without knowing the full story.*

"ShopMart was out, so I had no choice," she explained. "Anyway, it doesn't matter, because we can buy more now. We have plenty of money. I'll get my mom to drive me to Harris Fullers if ShopMart is still out, and we can get a few more containers."

"And blow all our money on overpriced supplies?" Amelia asked. She pushed her hair behind her ears, trying not to lose her cool. "Look, we need more of the right stuff. I'll take care of it this time."

"It's not my fault—"

Amelia shrugged. "Whatever. The point is, if we want to make a higher profit, we need to buy supplies at the lowest prices we can. You want to win, don't you?"

"No," said Resa, dripping sarcasm. "I'm in this for the company."

Didi walked back over and noticed the tension between Resa and Amelia immediately.

"Oh no," she said. "What'd I miss?"

"Nothing," said Resa quickly. "Did they have any powdered lemonade?"

Didi shook her head. "They said they're not

getting more until Monday." She looked near tears. "What are we going to do? Not just today but tomorrow? We need more stuff to make lemonade."

"We're gonna call it a day once we sell this cup," Resa said, trying not to sound as hopeless as she felt. "And then tomorrow—"

"I'm on it," Amelia interrupted. "Don't worry about tomorrow."

"What about Harriet?" asked Didi. "Shouldn't someone try to, you know, find her?"

"Can you guys finish up here and take the stuff back to my place?" asked Resa.

"Sure," said Didi.

"I'll find Harriet," said Resa. "I have a feeling I know exactly where she is."

~~~~~~

Just as she'd suspected, Harriet was at Val's lemonade stand. Business had slowed there, too—gone was the never-ending line, and a snoozing Clyde lay on a bench with his baseball cap over his face and his megaphone resting on his chest. Still, Giovanni and Val were working the stand, helping three customers—kids in soccer jerseys. The fanny pack around Val's waist looked really, really full.

Resa strode over to the bench where Harriet sat with Grace, doing a complicated clapping routine and laughing her head off.

Keep calm, Resa told herself. *Be nice.*

"Fancy meeting you here," Resa said, interrupting an especially loud peal of laughter.

When Harriet turned to find Resa there, she didn't seem the least bit embarrassed or guilty. "Hey, Resa!" She beamed. "How's it going?"

Resa took a moment to consider how to reply. She wanted to grab Harriet by her collar and march her out of there, saying, *Just what do you think you're doing?* But Resa was trying to be open-minded and a leader who listened. So she said, as mildly as she could manage, "Not great, Harriet. Not great."

Harriet looked concerned. "Why? What happened?"

Resa was perplexed. Could Harriet really be so clueless?

"Harriet," she started calmly, "have you noticed that you're at the wrong lemonade stand?"

Harriet shrugged and turned back to Grace. "I'm taking a break."

"Your ten-minute break," Resa said, trying not to growl, "ended two hours ago."

"Trouble in paradise?"

Resa spun around to face Val, but a flash of bright light made her squeeze her eyes shut. She squinted them open to find Val sporting a T-shirt with a gold-sequined sun on the front. The sequined sun reflected the light of the actual sun and was only slightly less bright.

"Wow, Val," said Resa. "Are you trying to blind us?"

"It's eye-catching!" chirped Harriet from her perch on the bench.

"Precisely," said Val.

"It's eye-damaging," muttered Resa.

"Don't be mad at Harriet," said Val, her voice sugary. "You can't blame her for wanting to be where the action is."

"No one's mad at anyone," Resa said with a tight smile. "Anyway, we've got to go. We can't leave Amelia and Didi to handle all those customers on their own."

She grabbed Harriet's hand and pulled her up, and together they walked to the corner. Well, Resa walked. Harriet skipped. She looked as if she didn't have a care in the world. It infuriated Resa, but she used every modicum of self-control she had to keep from yelling.

"How great that we have so many customers!" Harriet said.

"We don't have *any* customers!" Resa replied. "I was just saying that because I don't want Val to gloat about our failure! We're losing, big-time."

Harriet raised her eyebrows at Resa. "Sounds like someone is getting a tad overdramatic."

Resa had to laugh at this. "*You're* calling *me* over-dramatic? You're joking, right?"

"Why are you so angry?" asked Harriet. "You said you were going to be nice!"

"I am being nice!"

"No, you're not! You're angry at me just for taking a break! The break you told me to take!"

"Yeah, because you were screaming at the customers!"

"I was *trying* to sell lemonade!"

"And anyway, you said you'd be back in ten minutes, maybe fifteen! Not two hours!"

Harriet suddenly stopped walking and spun to face Resa. "You know what? I spent *hours* last night making that sign! Hours that I could have spent bedazzling headbands or perfecting my act for the talent show or watching videos of hedgehogs trying to climb out of teacups! Do you have any idea how adorable those videos are?" The more Harriet spoke, the more upset she seemed to get. "And then I spent alllllllll morning trying to sell your dumb lemonade! And for what? I don't get any thanks! Instead, I get criticized! And it doesn't even matter, anyway, because the stand is a flop!"

Um, yeah, because we're in the wrong location, thought Resa, *because I have to listen to everyone's ideas, even if they're dead wrong.*

"You have nothing to say, do you?" Harriet

stared at Resa accusingly. "You know what? Just forget it!"

Harriet spun on her heel and stormed down Walnut Street.

Resa started to follow her, then thought better of it. They'd only fight more, she knew. She took a few steps in the direction of home, but she stopped again. The last thing she wanted to do was face her parents, who'd want to know how everything went, and Ricky, who'd try to turn her into a chipmunk.

She stood on the corner of Walnut and Market, trying to figure out her next move. The breeze picked up, and a sweet aroma reached her nose. Something freshly baked. Chocolate-chip cookies? No. Cupcakes? No. Waffle cones.

The door to the ice-cream shop across the street was propped open, letting loose the tantalizing smell that made Resa's mouth water. She glanced around to make sure no cars were coming, then she darted across the street.

When life gives you lemons, make lemonade, thought Resa. *And when that doesn't work, eat ice cream.*

17

It was cold in the ice-cream shop, so Resa buttoned up her lime-green sweater. The smell of the waffle cones was even stronger inside, and Resa wondered how the teenage girl behind the counter could stand the temptation. You probably got used to it, she figured.

"Hey," the girl said. She had a unique and unexpected style that intrigued Resa. Her dress was gray, with buttons down the front and a white rounded collar, like something out of an old-fashioned black-and-white movie. Her wavy brown hair formed a kind of triangle shape—getting thicker as it reached her chin, where it stopped. Her long bangs grazed the top of her large, rectangular glasses. Her name tag read ELEANOR.

"What's your pleasure?" she asked Resa.

Resa turned her attention to the offerings in the cold case in front of her. There were so many flavors, and they all looked so good.

"I'd like a waffle cone," she said. "With, uh, I think . . . Rocky Road, please."

Eleanor rolled her scooper into the Rocky Road tub and deposited a perfect ball of ice cream into a waffle cone.

"Actually," said Resa. "I changed my mind. Can I have mint chocolate chip instead?"

The girl upturned the cone over the Rocky Road tub, redepositing the ice cream she'd just scooped. She rinsed the scooper, then dipped it in the mint chocolate chip tub.

"Wait!" said Resa. "Sorry, I just—I'm really sorry, but can I do the butter pecan? That's what I want."

Eleanor raised her eyebrows at Resa. "You sure?"

Resa nodded. But as soon as Eleanor had placed a scoop of butter pecan on the cone, Resa sighed. "Ummm, excuse me?"

"Lemme guess," said Eleanor, dropping the scoop of butter pecan back into the tub. "You changed your mind."

"I don't know what's wrong with me. I usually know exactly what I want. In fact, it's sort of what I'm known for."

Eleanor dropped the scooper into a metal cylinder of water, then gestured to a stool at the counter. "Have a seat."

Resa did. Eleanor leaned back against the wall, crossed her arms in front of her chest, and said, "So what's the deal? Your best friend ditched you? Your cat ran away? What's the problem?"

"It's just . . ." Resa bit her lip. Where to even start? "It's not a big deal or anything. I'm doing this group project, right? And it's a contest, and I really, really want to win. But it's just, the other girls got really mad at me for not listening to them, so I've been trying to be nice because I'm afraid they're all going to revolt if I put my foot down. But being nice isn't working, either, because we're totally losing the contest. Our top salesgirl screams at the customers. Our location is terrible. And the store's out of the supplies we need. I feel like I don't know how to do anything anymore."

Eleanor was so motionless and expressionless that Resa wondered if she'd even heard her.

Then Eleanor grabbed the scooper and said, "Last chance, or no ice cream for you. Call it in the air. What flavor do you want?"

Then, before Resa knew what was happening, Eleanor was tossing the scooper at her, and she was reaching for it, blurting, "Pistachio!"

Resa looked down at her right hand. She'd caught the scooper.

Eleanor smiled. "You, lady, have good instincts." Then she stuck out her hand. "Scooper, please, so I can get your ice cream."

Eleanor placed two large scoops of pistachio in a waffle cone and handed it over. Resa placed her money on the counter, then took a tentative lick of the ice cream. Yes, this was perfect. Cool and refreshing and creamy, with just the right amount of crunch.

"You know what you want," said Eleanor. "You just need to make a decision and trust it."

"I guess," Resa said.

Eleanor shook her head. "Nuh-uh, none of that. Do you guess, or do you know?"

"Yes," said Resa. "You're right."

"Hey, it happens to the best of us," said Eleanor. She scooped coffee ice cream into a sugar cone, then leaned against the wall in front of Resa and took a lick.

"Take my boss, Wendell," said Eleanor. "Nice guy. The nicest guy you could ever hope to meet, actually. Terrible boss."

Resa laughed. "Really?"

"Uh, yeah," said Eleanor. "Because he can never

decide anything. Three months ago, I suggested swapping out the birthday cake flavor, which no one ever orders—like, seriously, no one—for something new. I tasted this 'fireworks' flavor at this ice-cream parlor a few towns over. It's got Pop Rocks in it, and it's basically a party in your mouth. But Wendell was like, 'Uh, maybe. I don't know. We've always had birthday cake. Seems like a big change. Blah, blah, blah.' And then he asked, like, a hundred people's opinions, and he did nada. And so—"

She gestured to the tub of birthday cake ice cream, which was filled to the brim.

"Fireworks ice cream sounds amazing," Resa said, taking a bite out of her waffle cone.

"Of course it does," said Eleanor. "Because it is amazing. And we'd sell a ton of it. But Wendell's too wishy-washy. He won't take the risk. So look around, and you'll see how Wendell's business is doing. Saturday afternoon and you're the only customer."

"Yeah," said Resa.

Eleanor pushed herself off the wall and walked over to the counter where Resa was sitting. "If you're going to be in charge, you have to be decisive. And confident," she said, hitting the counter with her open palm to emphasize her points. "You have to take risks. But—and here's the key thing—you have to trust the people who work for you. Like, when someone brings you a really good idea—"

"Like fireworks ice cream—" Resa chimed in.

"Yeah, a brilliant idea like that," Eleanor agreed, "you have to listen. And then make your own decision about it. You get me?"

Resa popped the last bite of waffle cone into her mouth.

"Eleanor," she said. "You're a genius."

"Well," said Eleanor, "I mean, obviously."

"Thanks," Resa said, sliding off the stool. She knew exactly what she needed to do, and she couldn't wait to do it.

We gotta meet up. My house, Resa texted Didi and Amelia. Then she added, *I know what we're doing wrong.*

Didi texted back almost immediately, *Seriously? I just got home.*

Yes! Resa replied. *ASAP.*

K. B there in 10, Didi replied.

Can you call Harriet at home? Resa typed.

K.

The whole walk home, Resa kept checking her phone to see if Amelia had replied, but there was radio silence. So she was surprised when she walked through her front door and found Amelia sitting on her couch, chatting with Ricky.

Amelia looked nice and comfortable on the red couch. Stella lay curled up next to her, with Stella's head on Amelia's lap. Next to Amelia on the couch was Ricky's enormous book of wizard spells. Ricky stood in front of Amelia, in a wizard cape and hat, his hands in the air as if he were conducting an orchestra.

"*Mutata figura tua,*" Ricky proclaimed, "*cabra fieri!*"

Amelia frowned as she checked the spell book. "Close. It should be *capra fieri.*"

Ricky smacked his forehead with his hand. "Why do I always make the same mistake?"

Amelia laughed. "Don't be too hard on yourself. I mean, you're only seven, and you know way more spells than I do."

"But you don't know any!"

"Well, I know one now," said Amelia. "*Mutata figura tua capra fieri!*"

Resa walked over and plopped down on the couch next to Stella. The dog raised her head, and Resa thought she'd climb on over to her rightful owner. She didn't.

So much for dogs being loyal, thought Resa.

"Ricky," said Resa, "stop bothering my guest."

"I'm not!"

"He's really not," said Amelia in a tone so friendly Resa almost didn't recognize it. Amelia closed the spell book and passed it to Ricky with both hands. "But we have to work now, so how about I quiz you later, okay?"

"Fiiiiiiine." Ricky pressed the massive book to his chest and staggered into the kitchen under its weight.

Resa groaned. "He drives me crazy with the wizard stuff."

"Well, he's your brother, so he has to drive you crazy," Amelia said. "But as an only child, I think it's cute. I mean, it's definitely weird, but cute."

"So you got my text?" Resa asked.

Amelia shook her head. "My phone's out of juice. But after you left, I went into ShopMart and asked them to check in the back for powdered lemonade." She produced a paper shopping bag from under the coffee table and then pulled out four jumbo containers of powdered lemonade. "Turns out they just got some in."

"Yes!" Resa exclaimed. She grabbed a container, tossed it into the air, and caught it again. "Yes! Yes! Yes! This totally saves us!"

The doorbell rang.

"Come in!" Resa yelled, happily reading the serving-size info on the container's label. "In the living room!"

A few seconds later, Didi and Harriet walked in together.

"Good, you're both here!" Resa said. "We need to talk."

Harriet put her hands on her hips and glowered. "What'd I do wrong now?"

She didn't seem like her usual bubbly self. She had changed into black jeans and a black hoodie, with the hood pulled up around her face. Her mood looked as dark as her outfit.

"Harriet, are you still upset about before?" Resa asked.

"*I'm* not upset about it," she said, "but I know *you* are! You probably don't even want me on this team!"

Didi put her arm around Harriet's shoulder. "Of course we do!"

Resa got to her feet and walked over to where Harriet stood. "Harriet, you're right," Resa said. "I was upset that you ditched us for Val's stand. You can't do that."

Harriet's eyes widened. "I already—"

Resa cut her off. "But the whole reason I was upset is because we need you. You're our best sales-person. Of course I want you on the team." As the words came out of her mouth, she realized she meant them.

Harriet's whole body seemed to soften. The corners of her mouth tentatively lifted in a small smile. "So you're not mad anymore?"

Resa shook her head. "We don't have time to be mad. We have a contest to win."

Harriet let forth a shriek, then threw her arms around Resa.

"I'm sorry, Resa! I swear to you—" She pulled back and looked, hard, into Resa's eyes. "I will never visit Val's stand again."

"Okay, I believe you," Resa said with a laugh. "But, seriously, why'd you hang out there for so long?"

"Val's stand is super fun," Harriet said matter-of-factly. She pulled her hood down, unleashing a complex arrangement of hair. Harriet had pulled her thick, dark locks into two pigtails, then split each of those into a dozen skinny braids. The result was a sort of modern Medusa look.

Harriet plopped down on the carpet, threw her legs open into a straddle, and whistled to call Stella over. The dog bounded off the couch, and Harriet started scratching her with both hands. "Val's whole stand feels like a party."

Resa sunk into the couch. "How come?"

Harriet considered for a second. "The four of them called and texted every single person they'd ever met and told them to come. So there were all these people there, they had music playing, and it just felt like the place to be." She looked up from where she was scratching Stella's belly. "No offense."

"We should be doing that, too," said Amelia. "Getting the word out to friends and family, so we're not just depending on people who happen to pass by."

"Yeeeeeaah," murmured Resa as she mentally scanned her contact list. She could invite the kids on her tennis team, relatives, Ricky's friends, her parents' friends . . . Tons of people would probably stop by. "I can't believe we didn't think of doing that sooner."

"Well, we've been kind of busy," Amelia said with a smile. "Squeezing lemons, having a huge fight, fending off skinks."

"If we want the stand to feel like a party," Didi chimed in from the armchair, "what about balloons?" She kicked off her shoes and pulled her feet up underneath her. "The florist my mom works for sells helium balloons for parties and stuff. Maybe she'll donate some. The shop can be our sponsor."

Harriet clapped. "Yesyesyesyes!"

"And we should play music, too," said Resa. "I can bring my dad's wireless speakers."

From her position on the floor, Harriet gasped, then cried, "No!"

"What's wrong with my dad's wireless speakers?" asked Resa.

"Nothing's wrong with them," said Harriet, her eyes twinkling, "except that I have something way, way better."

"What's better than music?" Amelia asked.

"*Live* music!" Harriet exclaimed.

Resa immediately understood. "Lemme guess," she said. "Your brothers' band?"

"Yes!" said Harriet. She'd found a tennis ball and was rolling it across the room for Stella to fetch. "They'll grab everyone's attention!"

"Well, *that's* true," muttered Resa.

"They'll do it for free, if I ask," said Harriet. "And the best part is, they'll bring their fan base."

"Fan base?" asked Resa, trying to keep her voice neutral.

"They'll post about the gig," said Harriet. "And all three thousand followers will see it!"

"Three thousand followers?" Amelia repeated, dumbfounded. "That's . . . incredible. That would change everything!"

"Sure, yes, the publicity would be great." Resa felt as if she were losing ground and struggled to get her point across without making Harriet too defensive. "But we need to remember— Well, I mean, a lot of our customers are little kids, and the music is just, you know . . ."

She tried to think of softer synonyms for *nightmare* and *torture*, but she couldn't think of any.

"Loud," said Amelia, saving her. "It's really loud."

"Well, it wouldn't be the *Rancid* Skinks performing!" Harriet said, as if that should be obvious. "It'd be their kiddie band, which is just the Skinks. It's Joe on ukulele, Larry on tambourine, and Sam on harmonica. They hand out maracas. It'll be *great*. Don't worry."

"Who's worried?" Resa asked, and then she muttered to Amelia. "What could possibly go wrong?"

19

"Anybody hungry?"

The meeting was interrupted by Resa's mom, who walked in holding a plate full of steaming doughnuts covered in a shimmering pink glaze. Suddenly the living room was filled with a tangy, sweet smell.

Harriet abandoned Stella on the carpet and kneeled at Resa's mom's feet. "Mrs. Lopez," she said, bowing her head, "you are officially a goddess."

"Thanks." Resa's mom smiled. "But really, you're doing me a favor. I need to know what you think.

We're having a hard time choosing next month's seasonal doughnut flavor."

"What happened to blood orange hibiscus?" asked Amelia, selecting a doughnut from the plate. "Those were insanely good."

"We can't mass-produce," Resa's mom said. "The hibiscus costs too much."

Harriet picked up a hot, sticky doughnut, inhaled its intoxicating smell, then plunged her teeth into the dough.

"Mmmmm," she murmured, eyes closed in rapture. "Heaaaaaaaven."

After that reaction, everyone had to try one. Within half a minute, the plate was empty. Stella watched the girls chew with big, sad eyes.

"It tastes like berries," said Didi, taking small, restrained bites. "Raspberry?"

"Strawberry cheesecake, actually," said Resa's mom. "So I'm guessing the empty plate means two thumbs up?"

"I only wish I had more thumbs," said Harriet with her mouth full. "I'd put them all up."

Resa's mom laughed and headed back into the kitchen, where Ricky was shouting for help with his transmogrification spell.

Resa wiped the sugar off her lips with the back of her hand. Everyone looked really happy now that they were stuffed full of confections. She thought she might as well take the opportunity to make her announcement. They might not like it, but Eleanor was right, she had to be decisive. "Balloons are good, and music is good, but none of that will solve our biggest problem—which is we're in the wrong location." She braced herself for pushback.

But Amelia nodded. "That's my fault. I was wrong about putting the stand near ShopMart. We'd sell more lemonade in Siberia."

"It was a good idea," Resa said quickly. "It totally made sense at the time. And by setting up there, we figured a lot of stuff out." Now that Amelia was owning her mistake, Resa felt generous and charitable. "The best location is the park, where Val's group is set up," Resa went on. "It's in the middle of the neighborhood, and there's always tons of thirsty families walking by because of the soccer games. It's perfect."

"So let's set up there," said Amelia. "Across Market Street, on the opposite corner."

"Yeah, I was thinking in front of the elementary school," Resa said. "It'll be closed, which is good, because then we won't get complaints about the music."

"Okeydoke," Harriet replied from where she lay on the carpet in a full-on sugar coma.

"Didi, are you cool with that?" Resa asked nervously.

Didi gnawed on a nail. Waves of worry emanated from her. "Val's just gonna be so mad," she said.

"Yeah, probably, but we're not doing anything wrong," said Resa. "That corner's not her private property."

Didi sighed, then shrugged, then nodded.

"Here's the thing, though," said Amelia, licking strawberry glaze off her fingers one by one. "If we're going to set up right near Val's stand, we can't just sell the same exact stuff they're selling."

"We have to sell lemonade," Didi pointed out.

"Sure," said Amelia, "but we can think outside the lemon."

Resa raised her eyebrows. Was she hearing things, or was Amelia quoting her Idea Book?

"Signature flavors?" Resa asked. "But I thought they were gour-ross?"

"Tomato basil lemonade *is* gour-ross," Amelia said, wincing. "I'm talking about something simple."

Harriet rolled onto her stomach. "Strawberry cheesecake!"

"Cheesecake lemonade?" said Resa. "I don't think the world's ready to think that far outside the box. But strawberry lemonade could be great."

"That's perfect," said Amelia, nodding fast. "There's this big strawberry patch in my backyard. My mom and I have about a million berries we don't know what to do with. We wouldn't even have to spend money on extra ingredients."

Stella lifted her head from the carpet. She barked once, then again.

"Stella's on board," Resa said, grinning. She was feeling giddy with optimism. Suddenly it felt as if all the separate puzzle pieces were coming together to form a picture that made sense.

"This time," said Resa, "we mean business."

20

The next morning, all four girls gathered around Resa's kitchen table at 8:00 A.M. But they were not all awake.

Harriet was still in her pajamas, a fleece unicorn onesie complete with a hood that had ears and a rainbow mane. She slumped over the table, her forehead resting on her hands.

"You brought regular clothes, right?" asked Resa.

Harriet didn't move. The only reply she gave was a low groan.

"You know, Harriet," Amelia pointed out, "it

kind of defeats the point of being on time if you're going to be sleeping."

Harriet yanked the unicorn hood up so it covered her head. "Fimamanaaaaa," she groaned.

"I think she's asking for five more minutes," said Resa.

"Are you sure the balloons are okay?" asked Didi, pushing her glasses up. "It's kind of windy out there."

Didi had gone to work with her mom that morning, bright and early, and the florist had agreed to donate a dozen helium balloons as long as Lickin' Lips Lemonade put out a stack of brochures for the flower shop. Didi had been overjoyed—until she tried to carry the balloons to Resa's house. She didn't know how much helium was pumped into the cluster of twelve oversize mylar balloons, but she was pretty sure it was enough to lift her off her feet in a strong breeze. The walk took forever, and she had to stop every few minutes to untangle a balloon from a tree.

The balloons wouldn't fit through Resa's front door, so the girls tied them to the heaviest thing they could find and left them on the porch.

"The balloons are fine," Resa reassured Didi. "Ricky's wizard book weighs the same as a small building. They're not going anywhere. Come on, let's finish making the lemonade."

"Behold," announced Amelia. "The magical elixir."

She produced a mason jar from her backpack, filled with red liquid. She poured some of the strawberry juice into the plastic pitcher full of lemonade that Resa had mixed. The lemonade instantly turned an irresistible shade of pink. Even better, it tasted delicious.

"Mmmmmm!" Resa drum-rolled the table with both hands. "We're gonna wiiiiiiin!"

This, finally, woke Harriet.

She startled. "Huh? Wha? I didn't do anything!"

"Relax," Resa said with a laugh. "You're not in trouble. Get dressed! We're gonna win us some QuickTix!"

〰〰〰

Val's team saw them coming a mile away. The balloons were hard to miss.

"*Last day of the contest, Teresa!*" Clyde bellowed into his megaphone. "*You're getting pretty desperate, huh?*"

Resa shook her head.

"*Balloons will not save you!*" Clyde went on. "*Nothing can save you now!*"

Val's stand looked ready for a huge rush. They had a stack of at least a hundred cups on their table, and three pitchers of lemonade stood inside a huge cooler full of ice.

Val stood in front of the stand, wearing an emerald-green T-shirt with CHAMPION written in—what else?—sequins. Her eyes looked especially green, Resa thought—but were about to get even greener once the envy set in.

Resa and the gang slowed to a stop in front of the stand.

"How's it going, Val?" asked Resa.

"Well," said Val, stretching her arms overhead. "Not a cloud in the sky. Six soccer games scheduled for today."

She put both hands on her hips and cocked her head to the side. "The only question I have is: When the school counts up our money, will they throw in a private bus to take us to Adventure Central?"

Resa nodded as if she were giving this some real thought. "That's a good question, Val. I have another question for you. What happens to people who count their chickens before they're hatched?"

Val furrowed her brow as Resa and the girls crossed Market Street. "What are you talking about?" she called after them.

Resa could feel Val's team watching her team's every move as they set up on the corner across the street, in front of the school. They'd managed to unfold the card table and spread out the tablecloth before Val grabbed the megaphone from Clyde and shouted into it, "*What do you think you're doing? This is our corner!*"

Didi stopped smoothing the tablecloth and looked at Resa in alarm. This was exactly what she'd been worried about.

Harriet, though, didn't miss a beat. "*You own this corner?*" she shouted back. Her voice was about twice as loud as the megaphone.

"*Come on!*" blared Val. "*You know what I mean!*"

"*Actually,*" shouted Harriet, "*we don't. Because it's a free country and all that!*"

Then she unrolled the see-it-from-space poster. She'd added some finishing touches to it the night before. The blue feathers really made it pop.

Val's face was as red as her hair. "*One dollar fifty? Really? You're underselling us?*"

"*Maybe you're overselling,*" shouted Resa. She helped Harriet tape the sign to the fence behind them. It took half a roll of masking tape, but finally, it held.

"*Teresa Lopez!*" yelled Val. "*Are you declaring war on us?*"

Resa considered that for a second. Then she turned and yelled, "*Nope. Just trying to sell lemonade!*"

21

Business started off slow for both stands. Resa, Didi, and Amelia used the downtime to get the word out, texting, posting, and calling everyone and anyone. No contact was spared. It was a hurricane of posts and messages.

Customers trickled in slowly. Didi's dad came by in the first hour, with Didi's aunt, uncle, and triplet cousins in tow.

"Your mother doesn't want you to catch a chill," Didi's dad said, handing her a sweater. Didi tied the sweater around the waist of the yellow sundress she wore, which was covered in little blue daisies. It was eighty-seven degrees out, and the only chill she'd catch would be from air-conditioning if she wandered indoors. But her mom was a worrywart.

"How many cups do you want?" she asked her dad.

"Twelve," he said.

"Dad!" Didi laughed. "That's a lot of lemonade."

"I'm thirsty," he said. Then he leaned forward and whispered. "And you know the triplets have a terrible sweet tooth."

Amelia's mom was next. Resa recognized her right away. The resemblance between mother and daughter was striking—same straight blond hair, same blue eyes. But Amelia's mom seemed a lot more laid-back than Amelia—she wore holey jeans, a washed-out T-shirt, and a baseball cap. She also seemed a lot more social—she brought a whole posse of people from the newspaper with her, including a reporter who thought the fund-raising contest would make a good human-interest piece.

Resa was overjoyed.

"We'll give you full access—all the info you need, including our beef with that stand across the street," said Resa. "Wait—are we on the record yet?"

The reporter laughed. "It's a nice, simple, feel-good story. Can I take a picture?"

"Did somebody say picture?" Harriet asked, pushing to the front of the group. She turned up the collar on her shirt and tilted her black fedora down in a jaunty way. Before they'd left Resa's house, Harriet had changed out of her unicorn onesie and into her version of a power suit—fuchsia capri pants with a white-collared shirt and Larry's black suit vest, tightened at the back with a safety pin.

The reporter had the girls stand with their arms around one another, next to their massive, sparkly, feathered sign. Resa stood in the middle of Didi and Amelia, with Harriet kneeling in front, her arms spread wide as if she'd just finished a musical number.

The reporter was about to snap the photo when she stopped, said "Hold on!" and walked over to the stand to retrieve the pitcher of lemonade. She handed it to Didi. "Hold this. The pink pops—it'll advertise itself."

When the reporter finished, Harriet asked to see the photos. "This isn't my good side," she said. "And I'm not sure about this lighting."

Resa put her arm around Harriet's shoulder. "What my friend means is thank you. You too Ms. Grant—it was really cool of you to bring all these people."

Amelia's mom smiled. "Any friend of Amelia's is a friend of mine."

As Amelia's mom was leaving, a girl Resa didn't

know approached the stand. She was impeccably dressed, in the kind of carefully considered outfit you usually only find on mannequins in store windows. Even just the sheer number of accessories she wore stupefied Resa. She slid off her oversize sunglasses to look at Resa.

"Hi," said Resa. "Want some strawberry lemonade?" She gestured to the pitcher they'd placed at the front of the table, so its pretty-in-pink color could lure people in.

"Maaaaaaybe?" said the girl. "I don't know if I'm in the right spot—"

"*Cam-Cam!*" screeched Harriet. She torpedoed herself over, grabbed the newcomer around the waist, and, with some effort, since the girl was a foot taller, lifted her off the ground. "You came! You came! You came!"

"Ooooooh," the girl cooed. "You're wearing the cute capris and the adorable fedora! Yay!"

Harriet put her arm around the girl's waist and turned to face Resa and the gang.

"Guys, this is my cousin," she announced. "Cam-Thu!"

"Ah," said Amelia, nodding her head. "The giver of the umbrella hat."

"Ohmigosh, I can't believe you still have that old thing," moaned Cam-Thu. "That's so cringe-y. You must, you must, you *must* get rid of it. I have this all-weather trench for you—it's silver, and it's got a hood, and ohmigosh, trust me, you're going to love it."

"Eeeeeeeeee!" squeaked Harriet, squeezing her again.

"The hair, Harry," warned Cam-Thu. "Watch the hair!"

With just a few finger strokes, Cam-Thu summoned most of her school's debate team. They were a talkative and thirsty bunch. By the time they'd cleared out, Resa had to crack open the second giant-size container of lemonade to refill pitchers.

Cam-Thu and the debate team were only the first in a long line of visitors Harriet rustled up. All day, people walked up to the stand asking for her. There were the salesperson at Mr. Steuben's pet store; the pizzeria owner; the school bus driver; Mrs. Zangoli, whose hair was a perfect shade of Blushing Rose; the local dance teacher and her entire Monday tap class; two crossing guards; and countless kids from their school. Every time someone asked for her, Harriet would squeal, embrace them, and act like that person was her dearest friend, the one person she'd been waiting for all day.

"You think she actually loves all these people?" Resa asked Didi. "Or is she just a really good actress?"

Didi shrugged. "Who knows? But I think all

these people really love her, and that's kind of what's saving our butts right now."

Just after noon, Resa's parents, Ricky, and Stella stopped by. Resa was horrified to notice that Ricky was wearing his full wizard getup and had even put a tiny cape on Stella.

"Dad, this is animal cruelty," Resa said. "Not to mention sibling cruelty. Do you have any idea how humiliating this is?"

"To thine own self be true," her dad said, shrugging.

"I'm pretty sure whoever said that did not wear a wizard cape," Resa said.

"You never know with Shakespeare," her dad replied. "Hey, where's the band?"

"Late," answered Resa. "Of course."

"Too bad," said her dad, disappointed. "I was ready to get down." He did a fast dance move in place—a kick-y, twisty move that made her mom laugh and Resa turn beet red.

"Dad, are you *trying* to kill me with humiliation?" she asked. "Besides, Harriet's brothers don't play music you can 'get down' to. It's more like music you survive . . . Speaking of which, did you bring your noise-canceling headphones?"

"Yeah," said Resa's mom, pulling them out of her purse. "Even though I still don't understand why you need them."

"Just wait till they start playing," Resa said, hooking the headphones around her neck.

"Your pink lemonade looks great," her mom said. "I love how you put it front and center on the table. Who could pass by that pitcher without wanting a drink?"

"*Mrs. Lopez!*" boomed Harriet's voice. A second later the rest of her arrived, and she bear-hugged Resa's mom. "Get this goddess a cup of our finest lemonade!" Harriet ordered. She gave Resa's mom a conspiratorial wink. "Did you bring the goods?"

Resa's mom fished in her purse and handed Harriet a Tupperware full of doughnut holes, which Harriet instantly clutched to her chest, proclaiming, "I worship you!"

"But you girls need to eat lunch first," Resa's mom instructed, passing Harriet a shopping bag packed with food. "I brought sandwiches."

There was no time for a lunch break, though. When Resa looked back at the stand, a line of customers reached almost to the corner. There were so many people to serve that Harriet had to stop promoting and start pouring. It was all hands on deck—and even then, the line swelled further.

"Who *are* all those people?" Didi asked Amelia as she passed her a cup newly packed with ice.

"I just moved here," Amelia said, filling the cup with lemonade. "How should I know?"

She handed the cup of pink lemonade to a tall teenager with blue hair and a silver ring glinting from her nose.

"Do you know when the Skinks are starting?" the girl asked.

"You're here to see the Skinks?" asked Amelia.

"Uh, yeah," said the girl, as if that should be obvious. "I mean, why else would we be here?"

"So you're a fan?" asked Didi.

The girl chortled. "Uh, yeah, you could say that, if you're fond of understatements." She pointed to her hair. "I'm not as hard-core as the people who dye their tongues blue, though."

Didi and Amelia exchanged glances.

"The Skinks'll be here any minute," said Amelia. "Hang out. Drink lemonade."

The Skinks' fans did exactly that. By the time Harriet's brothers showed up—an hour late—the sidewalk was as full with people as Amelia's fanny pack was with cash. As the band walked through the crowd, which was peppered with blue-haired, blue-appareled, and, yes, even blue-tongued fans, a low chant broke out. "Ski-inks! Ski-inks!"

Resa stood on the sidelines, arms crossed, mind blown.

"I can't believe I'm saying this," she said to Harriet, "but I think you downplayed this situation. Your brothers have superfans. A lot of them."

Harriet shrugged. "Told you. You should listen to me every once in a while."

Resa pulled out her Idea Book, nabbed the pen from Didi's pocket, and scribbled, *Skinks merch. Custom tees? Mugs? Maracas?*

The Skinks set up an impromptu stage next to the lemonade stand. Joe, the front man of the band, tuned his ukulele, and the chant got louder. He shot the crowd a smile—or at least half of a smile. His sleek black hair hung down, hiding the other half.

"How we doing, Market Street?" he called, giving a little wave.

A roar erupted from the crowd. The blue-haired girl with the nose ring was shouting with particular gusto.

"You guys try the lemonade?" Joe went on. "Good stuff. Makes life sweet."

More clapping, whoops, and shouts of "Yeah!" and "Makes life sweeeeeeeet!"

Joe strummed his uke a few times, then yelled, "Who's ready to get down?"

Resa picked out her dad and shot him a look that said, "Not you, Dad."

The crowd was definitely ready to rock. Kids shook maracas furiously. Ricky used his wizard wand like a drumstick and played a beat on the sidewalk. Older fans screamed. They weren't the only ones screaming.

"*What's going on over there?*" Val bellowed into her megaphone across the street.

Resa just smiled and winked.

"*You're not having a concert, are you?*" Val shouted. "*You need a permit—*"

But then Larry started hitting his tambourine, hard and fast, drowning out Val's voice.

The concert was a smash hit.

A smash hit cut short, but a hit nonetheless.

As it turned out, the Skinks did need a permit. They were informed of this by a police officer who showed up fifteen minutes into the concert. Resa had no doubt as to who'd tipped the police off. The look of smug satisfaction on Val's face confirmed it.

Harriet tried her best to sweet-talk the police officer. "It's an unplugged performance," she reasoned. "Not even a performance, really, more like a jam session."

"More like a traffic jam," the police officer shot back.

"Here, have some lemonade, extra cold, on the house." Harriet handed the police officer a cup packed to the brim with ice cubes. "Did I mention this concert is a fund-raiser? For children in need."

"You children are gonna be in need of a lawyer if you don't shut this thing down right now."

So the show ended a bit prematurely. But it didn't matter, because by then, the stand was almost out of lemonade, anyway. They were on their last pitcher. As the crowd dispersed, the four girls gathered around the stand.

"Honestly, it's probably a good thing the show ended early," said Amelia. "I'm running out of places to put the profits."

Amelia's fanny pack had gotten so overstuffed with bills that she'd resorted to shoving the money into her pants pockets, and even those were getting filled to capacity.

"Do you know how much we made?" asked Didi. She was tidying up the table—tossing out dirty cups and napkins and smoothing down the tablecloth.

Amelia nodded. "I counted during the show. I counted three times because I was sure it was a mistake."

Resa's heart started pounding in her chest. The

thrill of victory was so close, it made her dizzy. "How much?" she asked.

Amelia broke into a grin so wide, it seemed to take over her whole face. "You ready?"

"I was born ready," Resa shot back.

Amelia paused to build anticipation. "Two hundred forty-three."

"Dollars?" asked Harriet.

"No, kopecks," Amelia said with a laugh. "Of course dollars!"

Resa let loose a shriek that put the Skinks fans to shame. Harriet, not one to be overshadowed, joined in—and then Didi and Amelia couldn't help but make some noise, too. Harriet slung one arm around Amelia and another around Resa, pulling them into a group hug, which Resa roped Didi into. They shrieked and squeezed and stamped their feet, and finally broke apart, laughing.

Resa felt all wound up, like a yo-yo being flung into motion. She danced in place and chanted, "We won! We won! We really, really won! So fun! 'Cause we won! Yeah! Yeah! Yeah!"

"What are you so happy about?"

It was Val's voice, but this time it wasn't booming out of a megaphone. She'd crossed the street and was standing right behind Resa, her hands on her hips, her green eyes gleaming.

Clyde stood next to her, megaphone still in hand. He lifted it to his mouth: "*They're happy—*"

Val snatched the megaphone out of his hand. "Seriously, I regret ever giving you this thing," she muttered.

"They're happy," Clyde said, "because their ears aren't suffering anymore, listening to the Skunks."

"The Skinks," Harriet corrected. "Get your facts straight."

"You're one to talk about suffering ears," said Amelia. "We all have hearing loss, thanks to your megaphone."

Resa laughed.

"Yeah, you're really funny," Clyde said. "You know what makes me laugh? The fact that you think you won."

"Uh, have you seen our cash register?" Resa gestured to the pack around Amelia's waist. "We shoulda brought something bigger to stash the cash."

"A laundry bag might've been big enough," Amelia chimed in.

Val snorted. "Gimme a break. You one good day. This is our *fourth* good day. I mean, how much did you make? Like, two hundred bucks? We had more than that when we started this morning."

All the air in Resa's lungs rushed out. She felt punctured, like a balloon. What Val was saying was impossible. The day had been such an incredible success. After adding Saturday in, they'd made $243 overall. After all that, how could they lose?

But if Val's team had a two-hundred-dollar head start . . . Resa's mind raced, calculating quickly. If Val's group made forty-four dollars today—selling just over twenty cups of lemonade—they'd be in the lead. And Val's team had definitely sold more than twenty cups. They'd had a long line all day— even managing to catch some overflow Skinks fans. Val was right. It was hopeless, Resa knew. It was over.

Resa's sense of defeat must have been written all over her face, because Val suddenly backed down.

"I didn't mean—look, you did a good job and all . . . it's just—"

"*Not enough!*" Clyde bellowed. "Ya lost, suckers!"

"Ignore him," Val told the girls. "The power of the megaphone's gone to his head."

"We don't need your pity, Val," Harriet said. "You don't know how much we made. And I don't see a fat lady anywhere."

"Huh?" Clyde looked confused.

"It ain't over," Harriet said impatiently, "until the fat lady sings."

"Oh-kay, then," Val said. She looked relieved to cross the street back to her stand.

As soon as she was out of earshot, Didi said, "She's

bluffing. I know she is. There's no way they started today with that much money."

Amelia caught Resa's eye. She'd done some quick math herself and figured out that Val was probably telling the truth, which meant there really was no way they could win. Amelia knew that Resa knew this. She also knew it was up to Resa to decide how she wanted to handle telling the others. Trouble was, Resa looked totally frozen, as if she had no idea what her next move was.

Didi, for her part, was getting more worked up. "This is just Val trying to mess with our heads," she said, nodding so vigorously her glasses nearly slid off her face. "I'm sure of it."

Harriet grimaced. "Uh . . ."

"What is it, Harriet?" asked Amelia.

"When I was hanging out with Val's group yesterday, they were talking about how much they'd made so far," Harriet said, her voice heavy with apology. "She's not bluffing."

Silence settled on the group for a long moment. Then Didi shook it off, speaking loudly in a way that wasn't like her, "Even if what she says is true, the contest isn't over yet."

"Totally!" agreed Harriet. "We still have an hour! Anything can happen in an hour!"

"We should all call our friends and family," Didi urged.

Amelia looked to Resa, hoping she'd weigh in, but she was staring at her feet, silent and still.

"All our friends and family have come already," Amelia pointed out gently. "And anyway, we're almost out of lemonade."

"So we'll buy more," said Didi. "I can run over to ShopMart."

Amelia couldn't let Didi blow any of their profits on more supplies—not now, with just an hour left. Harriet and Didi needed to know what Amelia and Resa had already figured out, but Amelia really didn't think she should be the one to tell them. She tried to nudge Resa along. "What do you think, Resa?" she asked.

Resa looked from Didi to Harriet to Amelia. Even now, they were waiting for her to tell them what to do. And she had no idea. The whole thing just felt like a massive waste of time. She wanted to sink into a deep, dark hole, or else spin on her heel and book it out of there.

"Hey." She heard a girl's voice behind her. "Did I miss the Skinks?"

The voice was familiar. Resa turned to find Eleanor in front of their stand. The surprise jolted her out of her silence.

"Eleanor!" said Resa.

"Pistachio!" Eleanor replied with a smile. She was wearing what looked like a vintage Girl Scout uniform—green and collared with lots of badges over the shoulder—along with knee-high black boots.

"The Skinks finished a little while ago," said Didi. "Permit problems."

Eleanor sighed and shook her head. "Ain't that always the way."

"Are you a fan?" asked Harriet. "They autographed some napkins for latecomers."

"Nah, I'm good," said Eleanor. "Larry's in my calculus class, so I can get him to sign a napkin anytime."

"Oh!" Harriet squealed. "I remember, you're the one who helps him with problem sets! He says he'd never pass calculus without you."

"Sounds about right." Eleanor laughed. "So what's this operation you've got going here?"

"Remember I was telling you about the class project? The contest?" Resa said. "Here you have it."

"Sorry to interrupt," Didi broke in, "but should we go to ShopMart? Buy more lemonade?"

"Uh . . . I just—" Resa sputtered.

Amelia jumped in to buy Resa some time.

"Hey, can we take a lunch break?" she asked. "I'm starving. Didn't your mom make sandwiches?"

"Yeah, that's a good idea," said Resa. "You guys take a quick lunch break, and I'll hold down the fort."

Harriet had grabbed the bag of sandwiches before Resa was even done talking. Didi and Amelia followed her to the bench on the corner, where they checked out the contents of the foil bundles from Resa's mom.

Resa turned her attention back to Eleanor. "Sorry, did you want some lemonade?"

"I mean, I feel like I'd be dumb not to have some," said Eleanor. "Since it makes life so sweet."

Resa scooped ice into a cup and filled it with lemonade.

"Maybe I've been selling lemonade for too long," said Resa, "but this pitcher doesn't look half full to me. It looks half empty."

Eleanor handed her a dollar and two quarters. Then she sipped from the cup. "This is one seriously refreshing beverage," she said. "Who cares if your pitcher's half empty or half full when it's completely delicious?"

"Yeah, it's good, but it doesn't matter," said Resa. "We lost the contest. That stand over there made more money. It's over."

Eleanor crunched an ice cube between her teeth. "Are you ready for a gem of wisdom?"

"I guess."

"If you guess, then you're not ready," said Eleanor. "My gems are too valuable to waste on the unprepared."

Resa laughed. "Okay, I am fully ready."

"If at first you don't succeed—" Eleanor said.

"Lemme guess," interrupted Resa. "Try, try again?"

"Bingo," said Eleanor.

"That's the gem?" asked Resa. "No offense, but, I mean, it's sort of . . . you know, cliché."

"You played hard," said Eleanor. "You tried a whole bunch of stuff. Some of that stuff didn't work—"

"Some of it was a disaster," Resa corrected.

"Some of it was a disaster," Eleanor conceded. "But you learned from it. You made improvements. You took risks, and I can tell you, from what I taste here—" She took a big sip, swallowed loudly, and made an "ah!" sound of satisfaction. "Those risks paid off. That's way more than I can say for my boss, who still can't let go of that birthday cake flavor no one wants."

Eleanor finished off her lemonade, sucking on the ice at the bottom of the cup. "So you lost," she concluded, "but you didn't *lose* lose, if you know what I mean." She gestured over to the bench where Amelia, Didi, and Harriet were doubled over, laughing. "They don't look like losers to me." She grabbed the pitcher and refilled her cup. "I think I should get free lemonade in exchange for my wisdom. Is that cool, Pistachio?"

"Cool." Resa smiled. "And my name's Resa."

"Ah, you'll always be Pistachio to me." Eleanor winked at Resa. "So those are my gems. Use them wisely. I gotta run."

"Thanks," Resa said. "And I'm glad you liked the lemonade."

"Life's feeling sweeter already," Eleanor said over her shoulder as she walked away.

Resa glanced at the bench, where Harriet was trying to toss pieces of bread into her mouth and missing pretty much every time. The crumbs that fell to the ground were attracting large quantities of pigeons—which made Didi extremely jumpy. Amelia sat on the bench, eating a sandwich and watching the whole thing with an easy grin.

Resa suddenly remembered that win or lose, they were all going to Adventure Central, anyway—and she was pretty sure they'd go together. They'd have to wait in irritating lines, sure, and they'd have to suffer the sight of Val's smug face as she breezed past them with her QuickTix and her dream team. But, Resa realized, she wouldn't trade her team for theirs. And suddenly she felt lighter. Her limbs didn't feel like cinder blocks anymore. Her lungs puffed up with air again. She felt a strange surge of energy that made her walk, then run, over to the others.

"Guys!" she panted. "We lost."

"You don't know—" Didi started.

"No, we lost, for sure, period. But it's okay!"

"Is this, like, a trap?" asked Didi. "Or a body-swapping scenario? You don't sound like Resa."

"We're not buying more powdered lemonade," Resa said. "We're not harassing our friends to come back." She grabbed a sandwich from the bag and unwrapped it. Suddenly she was starving.

"So what do we do?" asked Amelia.

"We celebrate," said Resa. She sank her teeth into the soft wheat bread. Turkey and Muenster cheese with chipotle mayo. Perfect.

"So you think we still have a shot at winning?" Harriet was confused.

"No way," Resa replied. "We definitely don't have a shot. But we do have forty-five more minutes and a half-full pitcher of the most delicious strawberry lemonade I've ever tasted. We do have a dozen jumbo helium balloons and a poster you can see from outer space. You need more reasons than that to celebrate?"

She took a bite of her sandwich and chewed while the others tried to make sense of what she'd said.

"So we just give up?" asked Didi. "Stop selling?"

"No, we keep selling. We just stop stressing," said Resa. "And we get the party started."

Harriet leaped to her feet. "You had me at party!"

23

Resa was right. Lickin' Lips Lemonade didn't win the contest. It did, however, come in a close second. Val's stand earned $288, and Lickin' Lips ended up totaling $252.

Resa, Didi, and Amelia stood together at homeroom on Monday, looking at the list of teams ranked according to earnings. Resa felt surprisingly pleased by how close the contest was.

"I still can't believe we made so much money!" Didi marveled. "Pretty much all in one day."

"*Winner, winner, chicken dinner!*" The girls braced

themselves for impact as Harriet hurtled toward them, right on time at ten minutes late.

When Harriet had finally relinquished them from her high-impact hug, Resa said, "Harry, you know we didn't win, right?"

"What are you talking about?" Harriet asked. "We won second place! In a way, it's better than first. It's less show-off-y."

She nodded in the direction of Val's group, which was clustered together in the front of the room, giving one another high fives and laughing.

"*We are the winners!*" bellowed Clyde into his megaphone. He was about to say more, but Ms. Davis's scowl stopped him short.

"I know you know bullhorns aren't permitted in school," she said, confiscating the megaphone.

Didi put her arm around Resa's shoulders. "I'm sorry, Resa," she said, giving her a squeeze. "I know you wanted those QuickTix."

Resa sighed. "I really did."

"Look on the bright side!" Didi smiled. "We'll have lots of bonding time while we wait in line. We can play games!"

"We can sing songs!" Harriet clapped in excitement. "I can teach you guys how to harmonize. No offense, but you need work."

"Orrrrrrrrr," said Resa, "we could use the time for brainstorming."

"Brainstorming what?" asked Amelia.

"I know we didn't win—" Resa started.

"We did win!" said Harriet. "Just not first place!"

"I know we didn't win first place," said Resa, "but we ran a killer lemonade stand yesterday. I mean, I think after we figured some stuff out, we worked really well together. And it was pretty fun, in the end."

"Yeah," said Amelia. "So . . . ?"

"So why stop there?" Resa asked.

"You mean, keep the lemonade stand going?" asked Didi.

"I mean, keep the team going," said Resa. "And maybe ditch the lemonade."

She opened her Idea Book to where she'd scrawled, *Cupcakes? Cookies? Personalized paracord key chains?*

"We could sell friendship bracelets!" Didi chimed in.

"We could start up a pet-grooming place!" Harriet squealed.

"Babysitting, too," said Amelia.

"The possibilities are endless!" Harriet said. "Just as long as it doesn't involve getting up before noon on weekends."

Didi laughed. "That kind of limits things a bit."

"We'll be like a club! A crew!" Harriet gasped. "A *squad*."

"The Starting-Up-Stuff Squad," Resa said.

"Okay, you're officially never allowed to name

stuff," teased Amelia. "Let's keep it simple. The Startup Squad."

Resa nodded slowly. "The Startup Squad. I like it."

The bell rang, and dozens of pairs of feet shuffled toward the door—Amelia's and Harriet's included. Nobody wanted to recite the periodic table if there was any possible way to avoid it.

"Consider this!" Harriet yelled over the racket. "Have you ever seen a dog with dyed fur? No, right? We'd be the only ones doing it!"

"Let's talk tomorrow!" yelled Resa as Harriet disappeared through the door with Amelia.

Didi looked at Resa and raised her eyebrows.

"What?" asked Resa.

"Nothing, it just . . . looks like I was right," Didi said with a smile. "Our group turned out to be great."

"I was right, too," Resa countered. "'Cause it started out as a total disaster."

Didi burst out laughing. "When that animal jumped on my head? He was so cold! Why are skinks so cold?"

She hooked her arm through Resa's, and the two girls laughed as they headed out the door to start a new day.

Welcome to

THE STARTUP SQUAD

You can start your own business by yourself or form a Startup Squad with your friends. It's fun! Resa, Harriet, Didi, and Amelia had a great time running their lemonade stand. The girls learned about *marketing*, *sales*, *location*, and *merchandising* as they worked together to sell their lemonade. Here are some tips from The Startup Squad that will help make your business a huge success.

Marketing is how you tell people what you're selling and interest them in buying it. Advertising in the local newspaper, making a sign to attract customers, and coming up with a catchy slogan are all types of marketing.

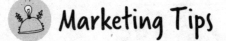 ## Marketing Tips

⭐ Choose a name for your product. It should sound fun but also clearly say what you're selling. ("Lickin' Lips Lemonade" is a great example.) You may also want to come up with a clever slogan that will make people smile and tell them even more about your product.

⭐ Make a big, eye-catching sign with your name and slogan to get people's attention and show what you're selling. Use bright colors and big letters so people can read the sign from far, far away.

⭐ Decorate your business so it stands out and looks exciting. Didi added balloons to their table to make it look like a party. Use a nice tablecloth, colorful streamers, fresh flowers, or anything else eye-catching!

⭐ Tell everyone you know about your business—and make a plan to tell people you *don't* know, too. Who might be interested in what you're selling? How can you reach them? Harriet told everyone she knew—and all the fans of the

Skinks! Ask permission to put up signs at places like your school or a local recreation center. Have an adult help, too, by posting about your business on social media, sending emails, and calling their friends and family.

★ Tell customers what you're going to do with the money you earn—especially if it's for a special cause. People feel good about giving money to charity and helping others reach a goal.

⊛ ⊛ ⊛

Sales means how you convince someone to buy your product. A good salesperson is able to confidently explain their product and its value.

 ## Sales Tips

★ Write out a sales pitch (a short speech) that will convince people to buy your product.

★ Rehearse your sales pitch like Didi did, until you can give it to anyone at any time. Having it memorized will help you feel more comfortable talking to people you don't know. If you're feeling shy, think of it like playing a part in a play. Act out the role of salesperson!

★ Look people in the eye when you speak with them, just like Harriet suggests. It makes you seem confident—even if you aren't!

★ Start your pitch with a simple "hello," "good morning," or "good afternoon." It's an easy, polite way to start a conversation that just might lead to a sale.

★ Even when you're not actively working on your business, tell people all about your product and why they might want to buy it. You never know where a sale is going to come from, so keep trying your pitch on everyone—and ask what they think!

Location. There's a saying that the three most important things in business are location, location, and location. Where you choose to put your business can make or break it.

 Location Tips

★ Choose a location with a lot of people. If you live on a busy street, your driveway, stoop, or front porch could be a great spot. Or try a friend's house or a public park. Whenever you choose, make sure a trusted adult is available nearby.

★ Think about whether the people in your location are able to buy. A location with a lot of people may not work if they can't stop to consider your product. You probably want people to be walking by, as drivers won't often stop. The girls tried setting up at the ShopMart—but it wasn't the best location because you can't take drinks into the store and people leaving are carrying a lot of groceries they need to take home.

★ You may need permission or even a permit to set up your business in a public place, so ask an adult to check the local laws. You don't want to get shut down like the Skinks!

★ Don't give up. Try one location, but don't be afraid to move to a new one if you don't get enough customers. The girls tried several locations until they found the best one!

Merchandising is similar to marketing, but the focus is on how your product looks and how it's displayed. How is your product packaged? What color is it? Can you see the product or just its packaging? How are you showing it off?

Merchandising Tips

⭐ Show off your product. If customers can see, touch, smell, or taste whatever you're selling, they're more likely to buy it. And everyone loves free samples! Just make sure those samples are small, so you don't give away all your inventory.

⭐ Think about packaging for your product. For example, is that pink lemonade in a clear pitcher so people can see its cool pink color? Are the cups you're using sturdy? Are they compostable and good for the environment?

⭐ Display your product so it gets people's attention. You want it to look desirable.

Oh, and one more thing: If you're going to open a lemonade stand, you need a recipe for lemonade! It's the juice from six lemons, six cups of water, and one cup of sugar. Mix it all together and you'll be all set.

Save or spend the money you make, invest it in your business, or donate it to worthy cause like a local food bank or an animal shelter. Go ahead, start planning your own empire!

Learn more about running your own business at thestartupsquad.com.

Acknowledgments

The Startup Squad was born on June 22, 2014, from my belief in the power of entrepreneurship and my desire for more positive influences for my two daughters. It exists today only because of so many people who deserve much more than just words on this page. (They should also get free bookmarks!)

First, thank you to all the publishing professionals who helped shape the original manuscript and to everyone who welcomed me and educated me about the industry. An honest thank-you to Norman and Joel for saying it couldn't be done; your direct and blunt words were exactly what I needed to hear at the exact time I needed to hear them.

Thank you to the hundreds of beta readers who critiqued the original manuscript. I'm extremely proud of those of you who were inspired to start businesses and I expect invitations to your IPOs.

A huge debt of gratitude to Simon Green for your enthusiasm and vision for this project from the very beginning. You made this book happen and deserve a free cup of lemonade from every stand you pass. (Just show the proprietor this acknowledgment.) Thank you to Anthony Mattero for stepping into Simon's shoes without missing a beat. And thank you to Jamie Stockton and everyone else at CAA.

To everyone at Imprint and Macmillan, thank you for sharing this calling and putting up with my naivete. The biggest Flatiron thank-you goes to Erin Stein—not just for saying "let's do it" eight minutes into our first meeting, but also for your vision about how to reach and impact the lives of so many girls. The titles publisher and editor don't do you justice. Thank you to John Morgan, Weslie Turner, Nicole Otto, Kathryn Little, Molly Ellis, and everyone else at Macmillan for all your hard work. Nicole C. Kear—thank you for bringing the characters and story to life in a way I never could have imagined (or done by myself). To Maike Plenske—thank you for showing us all what The Startup Squad girls look like.

To my girls—you were and are my inspiration and I could not have done this without your enthusiasm, ideas, edits, feedback, and support. Always know that this is for you more than anyone. I want you to have the entrepreneurial mindset, to always have your eyes open to the possibilities of what's next, to know that almost anything is possible if you work hard enough, and to never stop when someone tells you "no" (unless it's me or Mom).

To Hilary—to say that this would not have been possible without you by my side is a massive understatement. From your first "now what?" after I told you about this crazy idea, it was your support, always honest opinions, and much-needed edits that made this possible. Thank you for your unwavering belief in me. I love you, and I'm sorry for killing off Julie Rubin. She misses you, too.

Finally, my most heartfelt thanks go to *you*, the reader, for spending your precious time and hard-earned money on *The Startup Squad*. I truly appreciate it. Now go start a business. It can be a simple lemonade stand or a new business based on your passions. You can do it to earn money for yourself, for your family, or for a great cause. It doesn't matter. Just take those first steps and learn to think like an entrepreneur. Your future self will thank you.

In any business, and in life in general, you *will* fail. But the only true failure is not trying. So when you fail, just dust yourself off and try again. And again. And again. Then you will be a true entrepreneur.

Brian

Acknowledgments

My first and greatest thanks is owed to Brian Weisfeld for trusting me as a collaborator on this extraordinary project, his brainchild. Profound thanks to Erin Stein and John Morgan for their impeccable editorial guidance (and delightful demeanors), as well as to Nicole Otto and the rest of the Imprint team supreme, who make collaboration such a pleasure. As always, I thank my lucky stars for Michael Bourret, agent extraordinaire and protector of my career.

Grazie mille to my parents, Dr. Nicholas and Margaret Caccavo; my Southern family, Susan and Dan Greengold; and to Melissa, Courtney, Franca, Alanna, and Sidney. *Grazie a mia nonna Verusca, che si prende cura di tutto.*

To David, my dearest partner in greatness (and in everything else), thanks is perpetually owed. And to Giovanni, Stella, and Valentina, my inspirations, who give me all my best ideas, not to mention lots and lots of laughs and immeasurable joy, I offer mammoth mountains of thanks. When life gives you lemons, kids, we'll make lemonade together.

Nicole

About the Authors

Brian Weisfeld has been building businesses his entire life. In elementary school, he bought ninety-five pounds of gummy bears and hired his friends to sell them. As a teen, he made and sold mixtapes (ask your parents what those are), sorted baseball cards (he got paid in cards), babysat four days a week after school, and sold nuts and dried fruit (and more gummy bears) in a neighborhood store. As an adult, Brian helped build a number of well-known billion-dollar companies, including IMAX Corporation and Coupons.com. Brian is the founder and chief squad officer of The Startup Squad, an initiative dedicated to empowering girls to realize their potential, whatever their passion. Brian lives in Silicon Valley and can often be found eating gummy bears with his wife while watching his two daughters sell lemonade from the end of their driveway.

Nicole C. Kear grew up in New York City, where she still lives with her husband as well as her three kids, who are budding lemonade moguls. She's written lots of essays and a memoir, *Now I See You*, for grown-ups and the Fix-It Friends series for kids. She has a bunch of fancy, boring diplomas and one red clown nose from circus school. Seriously.

Meet a real-life girl entrepreneur!

Sara Robinson is the president of her business, Sara Sews (shopsara sews.com), and the winner of the Girls Mean Business contest.

SARA SEWS

Q: Tell us about your business.

A: We make handmade aprons for kids and colorful fabric party banners and sell them on Etsy and Amazon Handmade.

Q: How old were you when you started, and where did your idea come from?

A: I learned to sew when I was seven years old and started selling handmade doll dresses on Facebook, just for fun. Later, I added dresses for girls and dolls, aprons, and party banners. I needed a better platform for selling, and that's how Sara Sews got started.

Q: What's the most fun part of running a business?

A: Choosing fabrics and creating new products is lots of fun! I also enjoy telling adults and other kids about my business.

Q: What are your future plans for your business?

A: I'd like to move to a larger shop so that we could offer sewing lessons and open a market where other kids could sell handmade products.

Q: Do you have a role model or mentor?

A: I really admire Joanna Gaines. She has an amazing story behind her business. Her show, *Fixer Upper*, is one of my favorites!

Q: What was the biggest mistake you made? What did you learn from it?

A: I tried to make too many different types of products when Sara Sews got started. I learned that not every product will be popular and to stick with things that customers like, not just my favorites.

Q: Any advice for other girls starting a business?

A: Be bold! Do something that you love, ask for help if you need it, and don't give up just because you are young.

Want to be featured in the next Startup Squad Book?
Find out how at thestartupsquad.com